BETRAYED!

BETRAYED!

-⟜⟩➔ **PATRICIA CALVERT** ⟜➔⟜-

ATHENEUM BOOKS FOR YOUNG READERS
New York London Toronto Sydney Singapore

ATHENEUM BOOKS FOR YOUNG READERS
An imprint of Simon & Schuster Children's Publishing Division
1230 Avenue of the Americas
New York, New York 10020

Book design by O'Lanso Gabbidon
The text of this book is set in Hiroshige.
Printed in the United States of America
First Edition
2 4 6 8 10 9 7 5 3 1

Library of Congress Cataloging-in-Publication Data
Calvert, Patricia.
Betrayed! / by Patricia Calvert.
p.   cm.
Summary: In 1867, after his father's death and his mother's
remarriage, fourteen-year-old Tyler and his black friend Isaac set
out on the Missouri River headed West to seek their fortunes,
encountering an unsavory keelboat captain and Sioux chief along
the way.
ISBN 0-689-83472-1
[1. Frontier and pioneer life—Fiction. 2. Dakota Indians—Fiction.
3. Indians of North America—Fiction.] I. Title.
PZ7.C139 Be 2002
[Fic]—dc21   2001041257

Dedicated, in loving memory, to George J. Calvert

BEFORE . . .

Abraham Lincoln signed the Homestead Act in 1862, one year after the Civil War began. The new law granted 160 acres of land to any adult citizen of the United States for $250, or $1.25 per acre. The president's aim was to open the West to settlement as soon as the war was over.

Three years later, on Sunday, April 9, 1865, Robert E. Lee surrendered to Union forces at Appomattox, Virginia. The South lay in ruins. Atlanta had been burned nearly to the ground. More than 500,000 men in uniforms of blue and gray had died in bloody places with famous names like Gettysburg and Manassas, and not-so-famous ones like Wilson's Creek and Stones River.

The lure of cheap land was irresistible to survivors of the war. Men and women, young and old, whites—and sometimes blacks—turned their eyes toward a land where they could forget the horrors of the past.

However, the migration that followed produced a different kind of tragedy. Sioux, Cheyenne, and Nez Percé—to name only three of the many Indian tribes that believed the West belonged to them—were displaced from their homelands. Such tribes fiercely resented the intrusion of whites onto their unfenced prairies and into their sacred forests.

Not everyone headed west to homestead. For some emigrants, simple adventure was the lure. Such men often made the journey by water rather than cross-country, to avoid the wrath of the Indians. The rivers of the West had become broad highways of water after Lewis and Clark proved in 1805 that it was possible to travel all the way up the Missouri River as far as Fort Benton, in Montana territory. By mid-century, keelboats and later steamships regularly made the journey.

Sometimes those who went West were young indeed. Jim Bridger was eighteen years old when he boarded a keelboat in St. Louis and headed upriver. Kit Carson was only fourteen when he gave up his job as an apprentice in a saddlemaker's shop to begin a life of hunting, trapping, and exploring.

In September 1867, Tyler Bohannon and his friend Isaac Peerce found themselves shoulder to shoulder on a levee in St. Joseph. Before them, the Missouri flowed south to a union with the Mississippi at St. Louis. If they could find a captain willing to take them on, they intended to head the opposite direction—upriver, where new dreams could be dreamed. . . .

BETRAYED!

CHAPTER ONE

The wheels of Elway Snepp's wagon creaked as they rolled over the bridge that crossed Sweet Creek. Behind him, Tyler knew his mother lingered on the porch of the snug cabin where he'd been born fourteen summers ago.

In his mind's eye, he saw her hug herself, as if his leaving on this warm September morning had chilled her to the bone. To the right of the porch, Tyler could see the cowshed Papa had built the year before he rode off to war. East lay the garden where he'd put in many a crop himself after Papa joined General Shelby's Iron Brigade to fight against the Union.

Tyler longed to look back, to take in such familiar sights one last time. Why, he might even blow a farewell kiss to Mama. Instead, he steeled his heart and settled Elway Snepp's blue Winchester across his knees.

"Sooner!" he hollered, cupping one hand around his mouth. "Oh, *Soooner!* C'mon, boy, we're heading west this morning!"

The big red dog streaked like a flaming arrow down the slope where three apple trees, their branches heavy with a good harvest, were silhouetted against the blue autumn sky. The white bib on Sooner's chest gleamed as freshly as if Mama had washed it for him this very morning.

The dog gamboled merrily alongside the wagon, his red tongue lolling out the side of his mouth. Tyler saw that his brown eye was filled with eagerness for the journey, while the blue one reflected coolly on the perils that might lay ahead.

Devil eyes, folks called them, and got spooked at the sight of them. Tyler smiled. He knew better.

He sighed, then studied the backs of his brother Lucas and his sister Rosa Lee, seated on the wagon bench in front of him. Try as he might, he couldn't ignore the broad, not-yet-familiar back of the man who sat between them. It belonged to Mr. Elway Snepp, Mama's new husband.

If it weren't for him, I wouldn't be going anywhere, Tyler reminded himself with a twinge of bitterness. I would've gone on living at Sweet Creek till my hair turned white and my back got bent. Would've died a natural death, brimful of years, then been laid to rest up there on the hill where Papa's spirit was consecrated a few months ago.

If only Mama had held Papa's memory close to her heart forever. . . .

If only Mama had said, "No!" loud and flat out, to Elway's proposal of marriage. . . .

If only Mama hadn't set her mind to taking care of that brood of seven motherless Snepp boys. . . .

If only, if only! The hard truth was that Mama had betrayed Papa's memory.

Tyler felt drops of moisture gather at the corners of his eyes. He blinked them away and set his jaw. Shoot! If he was old enough to head west on his own, he was old enough not to bawl like a colicky baby over a wedding that couldn't be undone.

The marriage had been blessed by a preacher and witnessed by folks who'd wished the couple well. It was plain that Mama and Elway took the "till death us do part" part of the ceremony to heart. Trouble was, a new family had been created right in the middle of Tyler's old one, and didn't include him anymore. He became a stranger in the very place he once intended to live out his whole life.

A poke in his ribs from a sharp elbow reminded Tyler that at least he wasn't leaving Sweet Creek alone.

"Say, Ty, whyn't you tell me again the names a them places we'll be seein' out there where we be goin'," Isaac Peerce suggested. Tyler turned to stare into a pair of eyes the color of black walnuts, grateful to be jostled out of his reverie.

"There's a whole lot of 'em, Isaac," Tyler said,

pleased to hear no girlish quiver in his voice. Even Rosa Lee didn't cry much anymore, he thought, admiring his little sister's poker-straight spine and the way her dark curls gleamed in the morning sunshine.

"So tell 'em to me, then!" Isaac insisted.

"Well, there's this place called Three Forks, where Lewis and Clark found the headwaters of the Missouri River," Tyler began. Mr. Blackburn at school had helped him read up on the West, and Tyler recited the list as if it were a prayer.

"There's the Yellowstone River, too, called so on account of it flows over rocks that look kinda yellow as you look down at 'em through the water. There's a bunch of mountains called the Wind River Range, because the wind blows there most all the time. Folks claim that Jedediah Smith got his eyes froze clean shut when he walked outta those hills on a cold winter night way back in eighteen twenty-four. And—well, Isaac, there's so many other places—the Judith River and the Great Falls of the Missouri, and the Shining Mountains—it'd take me too long to name 'em all at once."

The brief recitation satisfied Isaac. Tyler saw the other boy's dark face crease in a smile, erasing the angry red scar on his cheek that traveled from his left eyebrow to the corner of his mouth.

Around them, the sun-dried fragrance of the bundles of hemp he and Isaac had helped Elway load this morning wafted up to tickle Tyler's nose. It even made Isaac sneeze hard three times in a row.

Tyler vowed never to forget that smell, because it signaled the end of one life and the beginning of another. The end of a life of growing crops like corn and beans and squash at Sweet Creek in northwest Missouri, and the beginning of a different one in a strange new country where some states didn't even have names yet.

As if he were a mind reader, Elway turned and peered down at the rifle lying across Tyler's knees. "With what you got there, I reckon a good hunter will be able to feed himself mighty handsome out in that wild land you're headed for," he said.

"I expect so," Tyler answered, feeling suddenly shy. He cleared his throat. "Thank you for letting me take it, Mr. Sn—ah, um—Elway, I mean."

The man was married to Mama now, wasn't he? Whether Tyler welcomed him into the family or not, he wasn't a neighbor to be politely called Mr. Snepp anymore. "I'll take good care of it, and if I ever get back this way I promise I'll return it to you," Tyler mumbled.

"Oh, I got a hunch it'll be many a long day before we set eyes on you again, son," Elway answered with a chuckle.

Son.

How hateful that word sounded the first few times Elway dared to use it! But now, knowing that Papa would never come home alive, that he was dead and gone for all time, it was easier to bear.

Just the same, Tyler patted his shirt pocket, where Papa's last letter rested against his breastbone. Papa would always be as near as his own skin, no matter how far from Sweet Creek this journey led. Tyler knew he was the true son of only one man—and for sure it wasn't Elway Snepp!

Yet when he recalled the trip he'd made all the way to Texas to bring Black Jack Bohannon home to Missouri, Tyler's heart felt bruised and battered. The journey had ended so much differently than he'd planned.

"It ain't right, what the Union did to us," Papa told him. His eyes were red-rimmed and slitted that final morning when they stood side by side on the banks of the Rio Grande at Eagle Pass. "I can't go home yet, Tyler, not till the score's been evened."

"But I came so far to find you, Papa . . . Mama and Lucas are waiting back home . . . even Rosa Lee, who was so little when you left . . . why can't you—" But there were no words powerful enough to change Papa's mind.

"Sometimes a man gets to a certain place in life because that's where his road leads him," he explained. "And the one I'm walkin' ain't come to an end yet, Tyler. I'm obliged to travel on it till it does."

It didn't matter to Papa that General Lee himself had raised a white flag of surrender on a foggy Sunday morning at Appomattox, Virginia. *Surrender* wasn't a word that Black Jack Bohannon would ever know how to spell.

Instead of coming home, Papa had followed General

Shelby's ragtag army across the wide, brown Rio Grande and headed for Mexico. The men of the Iron Brigade aimed to get fresh horses, weapons, and ammunition, then ride back across the border and go to war against the North all over again.

But months later (according to the letter that pressed against Tyler's heart), Papa's road came to an end sooner than he'd reckoned. He died in a fracas in a place called Brazil, so foreign sounding and far away, it seemed to be part of a whole separate universe.

Now, with Papa cast up there among the stars and Mama married to Elway Snepp, there was no reason in the world to linger at Sweet Creek a day, a week, a month longer.

Sneaky dampness moistened Tyler's eyes again. He swallowed hard and stroked the smooth walnut stock of the rifle lying across his knees. When the wagon lurched, his shoulder nudged Isaac's, rousing the other boy out of his own daydreams.

"Don't seem possible, do it, Ty?" Isaac whispered. "You and me heading west together? You white, me black. Equals, now that folks like me been e-man-ci-pated."

E-man-ci-pated. Isaac rolled the word on his tongue, savoring each syllable as if it tasted sweeter than candy. "Out there, it's going to be you for me and me for you, ain't it, Ty?"

"Sure enough," Tyler agreed. Slowly, it dawned on

him: The conviction that had driven Papa to far-off Mexico, then farther away to Brazil, now drove *him* to seek a destiny in an unknown place.

Strange to tell, it was Elway Snepp who seemed to understand best. When Mama objected about him leaving this morning, Elway had pointed out in a mild, patient way, "Ellen, maybe Tyler is like his papa. Some men aren't meant for safe pastures."

Aren't meant for safe pastures. . . .

Tyler shivered in spite of the sun on his back. He was Black Jack Bohannon's oldest son, never mind that he was as no-account looking as Uncle Matt, Mama's storekeeper brother. Tyler knew that safe pastures were not to be his lot, either.

CHAPTER TWO

The sun was three hours past its zenith when Elway halted his wagon near the levee in St. Joseph. Beyond, the slow-moving Missouri flowed by on its way to a union with the mighty Mississippi at St. Louis.

Elway peered at the sky, then drew a large gold watch from his pocket to check the hour. "We made good time, chil-run," he announced, then lifted Rosa Lee down from the wagon bench.

Tyler held back a smile. The first time he heard Elway pronounce *children* that way was on the morning he and Lucas and Rosa Lee walked over to the Snepp place to buy a broke-down, three-dollar mule from him. They'd named the old codger Patches, and prayed he'd have strength enough to make it all the way home to Sweet Creek. Tyler felt an unexpected stab of homesickness. That was only a year ago, when Mama was still a widow.

"You boys and Sooner keep an eye on the wagon," Elway said as he straightened his black jacket and took Rosa Lee by the hand. "This young lady and I are going to scout around to see if we can find us a hemp buyer."

Tyler saw his sister look up at her new stepfather with smug satisfaction. She'd been a mere baby when Papa went to war, which made it easier for her to cotton to Elway right off. Elway had his own reason for cottoning to her: Among his seven rowdy sons there was nary a daughter to call his own.

As Elway and Rosa Lee marched down the dock in search of a buyer, Lucas slumped against the wagon. He lowered his eyes and picked glumly at the metal rim of a back wheel. Sooner, whose thick red coat made him seek shade when the sun was high, found a cool spot under the wagon.

"Don't I just wish I was goin' with you boys!" Lucas exclaimed with a mournful sigh. His curly hair, the color of midnight like Papa's and Rosa Lee's, flopped across his brow.

Tyler stepped forward and looped an arm around his brother's thin shoulder. He regretted to think he'd been so lost in his own thoughts all morning that he hadn't paid any mind to Lucas's feelings.

"You got to get more schooling first," he reminded his brother gently. "Isaac and me, well, another year or two we'd probably have left to go off somewhere, anyway. We're just starting out a little early is all."

"Well, you two are mighty lucky to be headin' west on your own," Lucas insisted. He sighed again, as if he'd always dreamed of doing exactly the same thing himself. Tyler was pretty sure the idea had never occurred to him until this morning. It probably came to his mind the minute Tyler told Mama he and Isaac didn't plan to return to Sweet Creek after Elway sold the load of hemp.

"You just better believe that soon's I'm older . . ." Lucas's voice trailed off, filled with dreams and wishes. When his brother glanced up, Tyler found himself looking into a pair of eyes the color of day-old coffee. Both Lucas and Rosa Lee were lucky enough to come by Papa's dark handsomeness.

Doggone it! He got his own short stature, sandy hair, and freckles from Uncle Matt, Mama's brother. He was a steady and decent soul, and had been such a comfort to Mama after Papa went off to war, but for certain he wasn't a man to stand out in a crowd. On the other hand, what did dashing looks have to do with the kind of heart a person had? The suspicion that they did gave Tyler a moment's pause.

"Might be we'll come back this way someday and we'll take you with us next time," Isaac offered kindly, stepping up to loop an arm around Lucas's other shoulder.

Lucas brightened, and was about to say something when Tyler heard Rosa Lee cry happily, "Boys, boys! Elway and me found a hemp buyer!"

The man striding along at Elway's side was short and fat, had a face as pale and round as a cabbage, and chewed on an unlit cigar.

"You got yourself a fine-looking family, Mr. Snepp," the man remarked as they drew nearer, appraising Lucas and Tyler with a quick nod. "And I see you even got yourself a strong black boy to do heavy chores for you," he added.

"Isaac's a freed boy," Tyler said quickly. "Lucas and me do chores right along with him. Light chores, heavy ones, and every kind in between."

Elway steered the buyer around to the back of the wagon, causing Sooner to slink from his shady spot underneath and growl softly at the stranger's heels.

"I do b'leeve you'll find our hemp is first-rate quality, Mr. Pritchett," Elway said. He lifted up a bundle for the buyer's inspection. "It's well cured and ought to make the best rope or canvas a man could ask for."

Mr. Pritchett put on a stern business face and chewed harder on the cigar clamped between his yellow teeth. He narrowed his eyes, then tested a stalk by pinching it between a thumb and forefinger. "Um, mighta seen me some better," he murmured slyly.

"No, sir, I don't reckon you have," Elway declared. Tyler looked at his stepfather with grudging respect. Elway might look like a timid soul, as common as an old shoe, but he sure didn't have any trouble speaking up for himself.

How about the day that Elway drew his Winchester down on those two robbers who tried to clean out the cabin at Sweet Creek? Why, the scalawags even had a rope on Patches and intended to make off with him, too. That afternoon Elway acted like he was six feet tall in his sock feet and as ruthless as a grizzly bear that was waked too early in the spring. He'd been every inch Black Jack Bohannon's equal—maybe then some.

"Looka here, sir," Elway pointed out, plucking the stalks from the buyer's fat fingers. "Note how straight these are. Didn't grow crookedy or bent from being planted too far apart. Hemp's gotta be sowed close, you know, so each stalk races straight up to the sun." The buyer listened attentively.

"No, sir, the boys and I took mighty good care how we seeded our crop and how we harvested it," Elway went on. "I b'leeve I can get top price for this load, if you don't mind me bragging a bit. So if you're not interested, Mr. Pritchett, Rosa Lee and me will hunt us up another—"

Mr. Pritchett rolled his cigar stub from one side of his mouth to the other as if it helped him think better. "All right, all right! Since you aim to be so hard-nosed, Mr. Snepp, I'll give you top dollar. On one condition." The buyer studied Elway shrewdly with a pair of eyes as small and dark as raisins.

"Name it," Elway answered, his own glance narrowed.

"On condition you give me first chance at your next crop. What say you?"

"Suits me to a fare-thee-well," Elway declared. "Let's go yonder to get these bundles weighed, then we'll call it a deal." After calculating the price according to how many pounds were in the wagon, Mr. Pritchett retrieved a role of bills from an inner pocket of his coat and counted a sum into Elway's hand.

When the last bundle had been loaded onto a steamer bound downriver to St. Louis and Mr. Pritchett had departed, Elway heaved a satisfied sigh. "I was mighty pleased not to have to haggle overly much with that chap," he admitted. He checked his watch against the sky again.

"I see we got time to have a bite of supper at the inn up the street, chil-run. Then Lucas and Rosa Lee and I will be on our way home. You and Isaac come along, Tyler, on account of this might be the last civilized meal you boys get for a long while."

Tyler's mouth watered at the prospect of eating at an inn—the famous Oaklee Inn, no less. Never in his life had he been inside such a place. Rosa Lee got so excited, she danced a jig right there on the dock. But when they got to the inn it became clear they wouldn't enjoy a farewell meal together after all.

"We don't serve darkies here," the manager announced, without glancing directly at Isaac. How could he see Isaac if he didn't look at him? Tyler wondered.

"Isaac ain't no common darky," Tyler blurted. His cheeks suddenly felt as hot as stove lids. "He's a freed boy, sir. He's been emancipated and don't have to answer to nobody." The words weren't out of his mouth before he felt Isaac pick at his sleeve.

"Don't go makin' a fuss, Ty," he whispered. "It don't matter no-never-mind, honest it don't. I'll wait outside with Sooner. You just go eat with your kinfolk. Ain't no need to worry a lick about—"

"Free, not free, it don't make a jot or tittle of difference to me," the man broke in crisply. "We just plain don't serve colored folks at this establishment." He peered down his nose (it was a long nose, the color of a carrot), as if Elway should have known better than to try to gain admittance to the dining room of the Oaklee House with the likes of Isaac in tow.

"However, your servant can wait for you outside," the man conceded with a sniff. "There's a store down the way where you can get him some simple vittles, if that's your pleasure."

Tyler grabbed Isaac's arm and stepped aside. "You three go on ahead," he told Elway. "Isaac and me, we'll manage on our own."

Elway looked as disappointed as a hound after a poor hunt. "Hold on a minute, son," he said, and dug in his pocket.

"I'd planned to do this differently, but you worked mighty hard on that hemp crop, and I can't let you go off without paying you what you got coming." He laid several bills in Tyler's palm as, only a half hour earlier, Mr. Pritchett had put them in his own. "I hoped we could all say our farewells after a good meal and some apple pie, but—"

With their final parting only moments away, Rosa Lee began to cry. "We might not see you for a long time, Ty," she mumbled through her sniffles. "You better change your mind and come home with us."

"Or take me with you!" Lucas croaked.

Tyler gathered his brother and sister in his arms, which wasn't easy considering that Lucas was nearly as tall as he was himself. Rosa Lee's hair smelled clean as he kissed the top of her head, and Lucas's bones against his own were sharp and familiar from years of sharing a corn-husk pallet in the sleeping loft back home. Then he held out a hand to his stepfather.

"It was m-m-mighty fair of y-y-you to pay me, Elway," he stammered. It was hard not to feel nervous, knowing how he'd once loathed the man. He'd even prayed Elway would have an accident before the wedding—break an arm or a leg—so Mama would have time to come to her senses.

"I'll write from out there, wherever me and Isaac end up. Meantime, you t-t-take good care of Mama and these t-t-two here, and . . . and . . . say good-bye to Oat for me!"

Oat Snepp, Elway's oldest boy, had always been a mealymouthed pain in the neck, but it seemed polite to mention him in a farewell such as this.

Before moisture had a chance to collect in his eyes again, Tyler strode out of the Oaklee House. He gathered up the Winchester from under the seat of Elway's wagon where he'd put it for safekeeping. He hoisted up the bundle Mama had made for him, containing a wool blanket, extra socks, mittens, and a warm coat for cold weather. She had fixed one for Isaac, too, and with a nod, Tyler directed Isaac to grab it. Together, they headed back toward the wharf, Sooner hot on their heels.

"Let's see if we can find us a boat that's going up the Missouri," he informed Isaac matter-of-factly, blinking fast to dry the wetness that insisted on gathering in his eyes.

"Well now, I surely wouldn't mind if we got us something to eat first," Isaac groaned. "Maybe we oughta look for that place the man at the inn talked about, where simple vittles could be got. That lunch your Mama fixed—fried chicken and biscuits and all—was mighty good, but it's plumb wore off me."

"We will, we will," Tyler promised, "but first things first, Isaac. We don't have a horse or a wagon, and for sure we can't swim upstream to the territories. Which means getting passage on a boat is our best bet. Evening's coming on, and I don't want to let such arrangements hang fire till morning."

His voice rang confidently in his ears. He sounded like he knew what he was doing. The fact that maybe he did made Tyler walk a little taller. Because there was no turning back now. Ready or not, he and Isaac had crossed their last bridge in Missouri this morning at Sweet Creek. For good or ill, they were on their own.

CHAPTER THREE

"Looka there, Ty," Isaac said, pointing. "Ain't that one yonder prettier'n a peeled onion? Clean as a whistle, too, like somebody painted 'er only this morning!"

Tyler turned. Although it wasn't the largest ship at the dock, it was handsome indeed—a stern-wheeler nearly one hundred fifty feet long. It rode high in the water, and the name on its bow, *Undaunted,* summed up the kind of courage Tyler hoped would soon be his own.

A movement behind the window of the pilot house drew Tyler's glance upward. The man who came out to stand at the rail affirmed the ship's name. He looked like someone who wouldn't be daunted by the devil himself.

Tyler cupped his hands around his mouth and called up. "May we come aboard, sir?" The man stared down from beneath the visor of his captain's gold-braided hat. Tyler detected a faint sneer on his face.

"You may," he called back, his voice frosty. "Be quick, though, for I've got a lot of work to do before we depart at sunrise."

"Best I stay behind," Isaac whispered. Tyler knew the disdainful words of the manager of the Oaklee House were still fresh in Isaac's mind. He probably figured the captain of a ship as fine as this one wouldn't have time for darkies, either.

"Nope," Tyler declared. He didn't need to consider the matter twice. "You and me are traveling together, Isaac. Anyone who takes on one of us is goin' to have to take on both of us." He glanced down at Sooner. "Not to mention Sooner. We'd better make it clear right from the get-go that there's three of us."

Tyler and Isaac made their way up the loading ramp, Sooner following behind. The captain stepped forward and stood with arms folded across the gold buttons on his blue jacket. Up close, the scowly frown on the man's face made Tyler wonder whether he and Isaac—even if they got the chance—should sign on with the ship after all.

"It's about time you showed up," the captain snapped. "I assume you boys have a message for me from the Acme Dry Goods Company. Well, let me tell you straight out: If their merchandise isn't delivered and properly stowed by midnight, I'll be obliged to head upriver without it."

Ah. The only reason they'd been allowed on board

was because the captain believed they were carrying some sort of message from a shipper.

"No, sir, we're not from any dry goods company," Tyler said. Then, before he and Isaac could be dismissed, he followed quickly with an explanation of why they'd requested permission to board.

"My friend and I—this here is Isaac Peerce, sir, a freed boy who's not bound to anyone—want to sign on with a ship that'll take us up the Missouri. We aim to go where other folks are heading now that Mr. Lincoln's war is over."

The captain's lip curled. This time, his sneer was unmistakable. "You want to sign onto *my* ship?" His thick brows drew together in a solid dark line beneath the brim of his cap. "And, pray tell, what is it you boys can do that's so special I'd consider hiring either of you?"

"Any kind of chores that need doing," Tyler said. "Don't matter what they are. We're easy keepers, too, and know how to work hard. Why, just a couple hours ago we sold a load of hemp up the wharf there. Got top dollar for it, and like I said, now Isaac and me aim to go upriver where we can—"

"And I suppose you intend to bring that peculiar-looking dog with you," the captain interrupted. Sooner seemed to understand he was a topic of discussion. He gave the captain an affable doggie smile to demonstrate that he'd be a desirable addition on any ship.

"Yes, sir, we do," Tyler admitted. He wished there was time to explain how special Sooner was, that he was the son of a brave dog named Bigger who'd given up his life to settle an old debt and was buried now on a hill overlooking Sweet Creek. The captain's scowl advised him to hold his tongue.

"You talk about a load of hemp you just sold," the captain scoffed, his voice rising. "If that don't beat all the made-up, cockamamie yarns I ever heard!" His expression turned blacker than ever.

"I'll have you know I don't hire runaways. I don't carry contraband on my ship, either, as is the habit of some vessels you'll find docked at this levee," he thundered. "Therefore, be assured I'm not about to accommodate a pair of youthful adventure-seekers, not to mention a mutt that's got the eyes of a born killer."

The captain glared down at Sooner as if he'd heard all those tales about devil dogs. "Now you boys get on your way before I call one of my crew and have you thrown off," he ordered. "There's no place for the likes of you aboard a ship like the *Undaunted!*"

Isaac didn't need to be told twice. He was halfway down the ramp, Sooner skedaddling right behind him, before Tyler turned on his heel to follow.

"Lordy, lordy! That fella shore didn't take kindly to us," Isaac grumbled. "That business about you makin' up stories about the load of hemp—drat, that made me feel downright cranky!"

"Don't take it to heart," Tyler muttered through clenched teeth. "I reckon it's our good luck he told us to get gone." Just the same, it stung to have someone doubt they'd been paid for a long, hot summer of raising hemp—and even worse to be taken for runaways. *I'm running* to *something, not from anything,* Tyler wished he'd had the gumption to say.

"He's a sour cuss who most likely would've taken a cane to us if we'd had the bad luck to get hired," he said. He bent to rub Sooner's ears, then straightened, his shoulders squared.

"Anyway, you can plainly see that the *Undaunted* ain't the only ship tied up here, Isaac. We'll just have to keep looking till we find someone who'll give us a break."

Farther down the levee two ships had their loading ramps drawn up and no one seemed to be aboard either vessel. The fourth ship, tied at the very end, was a strange craft, unlike any Tyler had ever seen. It bore scant resemblance to the handsome steamers with their spit-and-polish appearance.

It was only half the length of the *Undaunted,* had no pilot house, and had never been blessed with a coat of paint. The heavy chain securing it to the dock was badly rusted. The name on the bow was painted in red letters edged in gold, much too gaudy for the vessel's drab appearance. *Darlin' Nell,* it read, hinting at a cheerful acceptance of life as its owner found it. No one was aboard it, either.

As Tyler was about to turn aside, someone called good-naturedly, "Say, there! What you two lads up to?" He and Isaac looked toward the stern. A round-faced man had just emerged from a small door in the five-foot-high, boxlike structure that occupied almost the entire length and breadth of the vessel. Smoke from the man's pipe swirled so thickly around his head, it was impossible to make out his features.

"C'mon aboard," the man invited amiably. "I been shorthanded lately, which means I been a dab lonely to boot. I could tolerate some company, boys."

Tyler exchanged a glance with Isaac. "If he's short-handed, maybe he'd be willing to—"

"This here ship don't compare worth a doggone to that other one," Isaac objected. "This'n don't have any style a-tall!"

"Since when did style get to be one of our concerns?" Tyler asked. "It won't cost us anything to find out what the old coot's got to say." Sooner wagged his plumey red tail in agreement, and was the first to jump aboard the *Darlin' Nell*.

The captain fanned away the haloes of pipe smoke that wreathed his head. Tyler saw his cheeks were rosy and his thick white mustache was streaked with brown tobacco stains. His small, twinkly blue eyes were cradled in pockets of soft, puckered flesh. Altogether, he looked a lot like the pictures of St. Nicholas in a book that Mama used to read aloud from every Christmas Eve.

"The docks of St. Joe aren't the safest place for strangers to wander about late of an evening," the captain observed. "Your folks know where you boys are at—or am I lookin' at a pair of runaways here?" Unlike the captain of the *Undaunted,* however, he said *runaways* with sly good humor, as if it were natural for boys of a certain age to light out from home.

"No, sir, we ain't runaways," Tyler said firmly. "My stepfather, Mr. Elway Snepp, fetched me here to St. Joe this very morning. He paid me for my share of a load of hemp he sold not three hours ago. Mr. Snepp—Elway, I mean—he's up there at the Oaklee House as we speak, taking a meal with my sister and brother before they head back home. Isaac and me, though, we aim to get upriver if we can find someone willing to take us on."

"Um," the captain murmured agreeably. He studied Sooner a moment. "And unless I miss my guess, you got plans to fetch this here funny-eyed dawg along with you."

"Yes, sir, we surely do," Tyler said without a moment's pause. Later, if he got better acquainted with the captain, he'd explain how brave Sooner's father had been, that Sooner had inherited his sire's great heart and bone-deep loyalty.

"And this lad here, this darky. I take it he's your servant?"

Tyler pulled Isaac forward so they stood side by side. "Then you take it wrong, sir. Isaac Peerce ain't nobody's servant. He's a freed boy, not beholden to man or beast. He'll work for himself, just like me. Now that Mr. Lincoln's war is over, Isaac owns his soul same as I own mine."

"And exactly what kind a work is it the two of you do? As you see, my ship's a small one. Ain't no place on it for them that can't pull their own weight," the captain said. He narrowed his blue eyes, suddenly all business, and didn't look as jolly as before.

"Any kinda work that needs doin'," Isaac spoke up. "Scrubbin'. Cookin'. Choppin' wood for that stove I see yonder a-top that cargo box."

The captain threw his head back and laughed, showing a set of ragged, tobacco-stained teeth. "Your skills are considerable better than the two scoundrels I turned down only this morning," he hooted. Something about the man was so easy and genial that Tyler couldn't help but warm right up to him.

"All right, I'm willing to take you boys aboard. Mind you, there'll be no pay. You'll get passage upriver and nothing more," the captain warned. "All I can promise is that if you do right by me, you got my solemn word I'll do right by you. I'll take you as far as my last stop in Montana Territory, way up there at Fort Benton, so far north, it's hardly more'n a stone's throw from the Land of the Grandmother."

"The Land of the Grandmother?" Tyler echoed. It sounded like a place in a fairy tale. Was the old man a bit soft in the head?

"That's what the Indians call Canada," the captain explained with a wink, "on account of it's ruled by England's queen, little old Victoria. So—does my offer suit you boys?"

Tyler looked at Isaac. Isaac stared back. "Suits us," Tyler said, speaking for both of them.

"Then you might as well stay on deck tonight, because I aim to leave long before daylight," the captain declared.

"I promised Isaac we'd get us something to eat," Tyler said, jerking his thumb in the direction of town. "It's late, so don't wait up on us. We'll just find a place up yonder to bed down, but I guarantee we'll be back before the sun's up."

"Fine by me," the old man agreed. "By then, the rest of my crew will be here as well. And by the by, I'm Captain Richard Little. And you boys are—"

"Tyler Bohannon, from Sweet Creek, Missouri," Tyler said, "and like I said a minute ago, this here is Isaac Peerce." He stuck his hand out, to seal the agreement with a shake. Captain Little's grip was mild and soft, not a knuckle-buster like Tyler knew he'd have gotten from the captain of the *Undaunted* if they'd gotten to the handshake stage.

"See you lads before daybreak, then," Richard Little said, his blue eyes twinkling merrily. "But before you go—what d'you call this here red-as-blazes dawg?"

"Sooner," Isaac said proudly. Before the captain

could remark about Sooner's eyes, he added, "Folks think he's blind in that light eye, or it means he's a devil dog. Neither one, sir. He inherited that blue one from his ancestors. Highland sheep dogs they were, from way over there in Scotland."

The captain dropped his hand lightly onto Sooner's head, and got a brisk tail wag in reply. A good sign, Tyler decided, because Sooner usually wasn't shy about letting people know he didn't like them—those two thieves back at Sweet Creek or the hemp buyer, for instance.

Tyler and Isaac turned back toward town, when Tyler suddenly whirled to face Captain Little. "If you don't mind, sir, what kind of a boat is this?" he asked.

"An old one!" The captain guffawed, as if the answer were witty. Richard Little knocked the ashes from his pipe before he went on. "This here's a keelboat, laddie. Built in Pittsburgh in eighteen fifty-three and cost three thousand dollars new. As your eyes will tell you, *Nell's* been up and down many a river since then." He paused and tucked the empty pipe into the pocket of his jacket.

"She's got a draft of only twenty-four inches, meaning she rides light as a leaf on the water. Her breadth of beam is eighteen feet, she carries fifteen to twenty tons of cargo, and runs with a crew of ten. *Nell's* powered by everything but steam, and she's been sweeter to me than a good wife could ever be. Now, see you in the morning—agreed?"

"Agreed," Tyler said.

As they turned back toward the twilit streets of St.

Joe, Isaac leaned close. "Powered by ever'thing but steam? What d'you reckon he means, Ty?" he asked suspiciously.

"Beats me," Tyler admitted. "But we'll find out soon enough. Right now, let's get something to eat, since you claim to be starved near to death."

Then, remembering the list of skills Isaac had mentioned to Captain Little, Tyler gave Isaac a light punch on the arm.

"You witless fool! Why'd you tell Captain Little we could *cook,* for lordy sakes?"

But Isaac was too excited to take the reprimand to heart. "We got us passage, Ty!" he exclaimed. "Even if it's only on a tub. Just think, in the morning, we'll be heading up that big old brown river. . . ." Isaac paused, as if realizing what it meant. In the falling darkness he fixed Tyler with an awed gaze.

"Afterward, we won't be boys no more, Ty," Isaac whispered. "We'll be all growed up. We'll be men!"

We'll be men. . . .

The prediction sent a thrill of hope and fear through every bone in Tyler's body. Up the street, he saw the lights of the Oaklee House glowing cheerily in the blue September dusk.

Elway's wagon was gone from out front where it had been tied. Tomorrow he and Isaac and Sooner would head up a watery trail called the Missouri, and even though the September air was mild, Tyler felt strangely chilled.

CHAPTER FOUR

The owner of the vittles store was about to hang a CLOSED sign in his window when Tyler and Isaac arrived.

"Another minute and you'd have been outta luck," he grumbled, wiping his hands on a stained white apron. "Do your shopping quick, boys, on account of I got supper waiting for me on the stove at home."

Tyler and Isaac hastily picked out a dozen hard bisquits, several slices of cured meat from a glass case, a stout wedge of yellow cheese, and three apples. Tyler gave a long look at the penny candy that glowed like green and red and yellow gems in fat glass jars on the counter. He turned his glance aside. Such treats belonged to a life he and Isaac were leaving behind.

Outside the store the boys settled themselves on a bench along the broadwalk, then Isaac greedily unwrapped the meat. They tore open the biscuits and stuffed slices of ham and chunks of cheese between the halves. They ate ravenously, like a pair of wolves, not saying a word until only four biscuits, a few pieces of meat, and some crumbles of cheese were left.

"We'll keep the rest for breakfast—and save part of that biscuit you're chompin' on," Tyler said, holding back a portion of his own. "Sooner's got to have some supper, too."

Tyler held out a section of his last biscuit to Sooner, who swallowed it so quick, he couldn't have tasted it. Isaac studied his own final portion regretfully, sighed, and did the same.

"A cup a your mama's coffee an' her raisin pie sure would taste fine right now," he said when they'd finished eating an apple apiece.

"Except her coffee and pie are miles away, being drunk and et by others than you and me," Tyler answered matter-of-factly. By Oat Snepp and his six little brothers, no less. Tyler pictured those boys hunched around his mother's supper table, their eyes shiny and grateful in the lamplight. For a moment he felt more like an outcast than ever.

"Anyway, dessert's the least of our concerns," he said, determined not to dwell on what he'd given up. "We told Captain Little not to wait on us, so we'd better rustle up a place to catch a few winks before morning comes."

"Shoot, that old feller'd let us back on his boat in a Missouri minute," Isaac pointed out. "Why don't we just hike back down there and—"

"Aw, it's too late now," Tyler objected. "He's probably got himself all settled for the night. We can find a place on our own." He squinted at a sign down the street. It was barely readable in the evening gloom. "'Beds. Clean. Fifteen cents a nite,'" he read aloud.

No doubt the owners of such an establishment would object to Isaac as rudely as the man at the inn had. They'd probably order him out back to sleep in the woodshed. Well, if Isaac had to sleep in a shed, that's where he'd sleep himself, Tyler decided.

"All I can say is we best find something quick," Isaac said, yawning mightily, "on account of this mama's boy be tired enough to fall asleep on his feet." He peered up and down the darkening street. "'Cept I sure don't see a likely place anywheres, Ty. Why not give a second thought to goin' back to the levee?"

"No one'll see us if we sneak around to the back of that livery stable at the end of the next block," Tyler suggested. "We'll find us an empty stall with some clean hay and hunker down till we meet up with Captain Little in the morning."

Isaac chuckled softly. "Bet you never slept wit' horses an' mules before, white boy. Isaac be plenty used to it, though. Can get cold sometimes, but with three of us it oughta be easy to stay warm."

Tyler wagged his finger under Isaac's nose. "Whoa! Remember that day back at Sweet Creek? We agreed you wouldn't call me white boy no more." Isaac nodded, but Tyler thought his smile was amused.

They found a stall close to the back entrance of Wilson & McGillicuddy's First-Rate Livery, the better to flee in case anyone found them. Although it was almost too dark to see, they arranged the hay to their satisfaction, even plumping up mounds for pillows. Before Isaac nestled down, Tyler announced that they needed to take care of some unfinished business.

"Bizness?" Isaac echoed. "What kind a bizness, Ty?" Tyler saw a look of apprehension in the other boy's dark eyes. Did Isaac suppose he was going to be asked to sleep in a nearby stall by himself? Tyler wondered.

"It ain't nothing bad, Isaac, so don't go getting spooked," Tyler said. Funny. You could think you knew a person, then something like this made you realize you didn't. The other person might be plagued by memories of bad luck and poor treatment that he couldn't tell you about. All you knew was that the experiences had left him permanently suspicious.

"The business I'm talking about is what I owe you for the work you done with that hemp," Tyler explained. "Planting it. Harvesting it. Helping load it this morning for the trip down here to St. Joe."

Tyler reached into his trousers and drew out the money Elway had given him. "Elway paid me, Isaac, now it's my turn to pay you." He held several bills out to Isaac. "Does that look about right to you?" he asked.

Isaac took the money and peered down at it. "You goin' to . . . *pay* me?" His usually thick, dark voice was thin and pale with amazement.

"Lordy, ain't you ever been paid money before?" Tyler asked. Once he'd worked for Uncle Matt for two weeks and got four dollars. Before that—before the war started, when he was only eight years old—Papa gave him two dollars for chopping enough wood to last till Thanksgiving.

"Never once," Isaac admitted softly. "I got fed. Most times I had a roof over my head. Nobody ever paid me nothin', though. I s'pose folks figgered a black boy with money in his pocket would run off quicker'n a scalded hog." He glanced up with a sheepish smile.

"'Cept you know I can't count, Ty. You could cheat ol' Isaac blind an' he'd never know the diff'rence."

"You know I ain't about to cheat you, Isaac," Tyler chided. "You got twenty dollars there, almost half what Elway gave me. I kept back a little extra for myself on account of it was my papa's land that hemp was growed on. Seemed fair to me, but if you got any complaints, speak up now and we'll argue it out."

He watched as Isaac tucked the bills into his pants pocket as reverently as if they were two hundred instead of twenty. "No complaints, Ty," Isaac said, his voice full of wonder. "No arguments, neither. Nary a one."

They lay down silently in the dark, with Sooner snuggled cozily in between. For a while they strained their ears for the sound of footsteps in the stable aisles, but there was only the rustle of hay in nearby stalls as horses ate or shifted their weight. In a few moments, the night beyond the open door at the end of the stable turned blacker than printer's ink.

"Does it scare you, Isaac?" Tyler murmured into the darkness over his head. "I mean, you and me goin' so far away? Getting so far from anything that looks like home?"

But Isaac was already asleep. Even Sooner was snoring lightly. Tyler turned on his side and pressed his backbone closer to Sooner's warm carcass. He closed his fingers around the cold barrel of Elway's Winchester.

"Don't seem it's really me—skinny ol' Tyler Bohannon—that's doing this," he whispered to himself. He had vowed to live and die surrounded by the mild green hills of Sweet Creek, a place that once seemed like paradise, yet here he was.

The truth was, paradise was a time before Mama married Elway. Before she decided to be a mother to those seven scrappy Snepp boys. Now there wasn't room for him at Sweet Creek, leastways not as the man of the house, which is what he'd been after Papa went away. So it was fitting that tomorrow he and Isaac and Sooner would board the *Darlin' Nell* and leave Missouri behind. Forever, maybe.

• • •

Tyler stirred long before the sun was up. Cool, foggy air drifted through the stalls. Instead of being inky, the open door at the end of the stable was a charcoal-colored rectangle. Tyler reached across Sooner and joggled Isaac's shoulder.

"Wake up, Isaac," he whispered. "We'll eat the rest of that meat and cheese and share our last apple before we go meet Captain Little. And don't forget to save a bite for Sooner."

The three of them gobbled up the remainder of the food. Tyler ate on one side of the apple, then passed it to Isaac, who ate on the opposite side. They washed everything down with water gathered in their cupped hands from a pump next to the horse trough outside. Sooner took time to lift his leg and leave his mark on the end posts of several stalls. To make Elway's Winchester less conspicuous, Tyler carried it under his bundle of clothes, then they slid silently into the gray light.

It was so early that the steamships at the levee were still dark and silent, even the *Undaunted*. From one of the square openings in the low-slung cargo box on the *Darlin' Nell*, however, a faint gleam of lantern light could be seen. Captain Little climbed out onto the narrow walkway, prying sleep out of his eyes. He whacked his knee when he saw the threesome on the dock.

"Why, I never expected to see you boys again, not to mention that weird-eyed pooch!" he admitted with a chuckle. "Figured I probably dreamed you up, or at the very least you'd have second thoughts and head home to join up with that hemp-growin' stepdaddy you mentioned."

Captain Little stretched mightily fore and aft, as Sooner had done half an hour earlier. He combed his wild white mane with dirty fingers before resettling his cap. Its visor wasn't polished, as it was on the hat of the captain of the *Undaunted,* nor did it boast any gold braid.

"Step up here, lads," Captain Little invited. "There's a small cook fire going atop the cargo box, and I got a pot of coffee brewing. You got a thirst for some, darker'n tar though it is?"

Tyler glanced at the wooden top of the cargo box. Was the captain crazy? He was taking a chance on burning up his vessel before it even pulled away from the levee! Then he noticed the fire had been built in a four-legged metal contraption about the size of a small washtub. Beneath it, a thick bed of river sand, held in place by a ring of smooth stones, insulated the wooden top of the box against the heat.

Tyler and Isaac stepped on board. As they did, Tyler realized what he'd taken to be bundles of freight lying against the side of the cargo box were actually three sleeping men. Another lay nearby, and in a square space at the bow of the vessel four more motionless lumps could be seen in the gray gloom. But hadn't the captain said yesterday that he carried a crew of ten?

The other two will be along shortly," Captain Little explained. "They wanted to hoist a few glasses of courage at the No More Chances last night, but I told 'em to be here before sunup."

Using a ladder nailed to the side of the cargo box, the captain clambered atop. He filled two dented tin mugs with a brew that was blacker than night had been a few hours ago, and handed them down to Tyler and Isaac. "Got no sugar or milk to go with it, laddies," he joshed, "because I surely wouldn't want you to get the notion this was goin' to be some kind of pleasure trip."

The captain plucked his pipe from his pocket and filled it with fresh tobacco. Soon a blue wreath of fragrant smoke encircled his head.

"Got all my merchandise loaded last night, so I reckon it's time to be waking these other chaps." With the toe of one foot he nudged each of the inert lumps next to the cargo box, then went forward to the ship's bow to do the same.

"Time to face the music, boys," Captain Little announced. "Everyone on your feet, for I want to put this vessel out before those steamers hog the waterway and set the waves washin' over our bow." The captain gestured up the dock to where the other vessels dozed at the wharf.

"It'll take those boys a while to work up a good head of steam," he explained, "whereas we can sneak away as quick and quiet as you please. Which is exactly the way I always leave a dock."

Tyler cleared his throat. Last night, before sleep came, he'd thought of another question that begged for an answer. "Can I ask what you're carrying, sir?" Maybe he wasn't entitled to know. If so, Captain Little would be quick to tell him to mind his own business.

"All the things those red folks upriver hanker after," Captain Little said, his twinkling blue eyes and cheerful grin once again reminding Tyler of St. Nicholas.

"I didn't know Indians had money to buy anything!" Tyler exclaimed.

"Money? My no, sonny, those red folks don't have money. What they do is trade back with me. I swap what I got to them, and they swap what they got right back. It ain't money that changes hands—it's goods."

Tyler was just as startled to know Indians had stuff to trade. They had horses, of course. But how could the captain haul away a half dozen wild ponies on a keelboat? His puzzlement must've registered on his face, because Captain Little hooted impatiently. "Why, they got robes and furs, boy!"

Tyler imagined the robes worn by French kings and queens in the history book Mr. Blackburn once showed the class back home. Robes that swept the floor and were trimmed with ermine tails.

"Buffalo robes, sonny, not the kind you're thinkin' about!" Captain Little said, as if he saw the images passing through Tyler's head.

"Yes, sir, people back east are plumb crazy about

buffalo robes, especially now that they're gettin' in short supply. Will pay a hunert dollars or more for a good one. Not to mention those red folks got beaver and mink and otter pelts to swap. Rich ladies like such fancy stuff to trim their coats—rich men, too, far as that goes."

Tyler nodded. He'd seen lots of otters in the creek back home but he couldn't imagine wearing one around his neck.

"The Indians are happy to trade because they want what they know I got," the captain went on. "Which includes pots and pans just like your mama uses. Why, they'll trade me for any old battered tin thing that don't have a hole in the bottom!"

Captain Little brushed away the turban of pipe smoke that wrapped his head. "They swap for knives and scissors and sewing needles, too, not to mention bolts of calico—red and blue and green and yellow—the brighter the better. And I got colored bangles and beads by the bushel basket," he reported gleefully. "Them pretties cost me next to nothin' in St. Louis, but you'd think they was solid gold the way those Indian girls line up to get 'em."

"Ah, kin I ask a question, sir?" Isaac spoke up.

Tyler and Captain Little turned to him in surprise, as if they'd forgotten Isaac had a tongue and could speak for himself. "Why, surely. What's on your mind?"

"Those red folk . . . um . . . are they really *red*?"

Captain Little slapped his knee again. "Not a

mother's one of 'em! In fact, I've met some that were fair—not as pale as your chum Tyler here—but light skinned just the same. Some are dark brown—not as black as you, of course—and most are somewhere in between."

"So why do folks say they're red if they ain't?" Isaac persisted.

"On account of back more'n a hundred years ago, French explorers called those folks *peaux rouges,* or 'redskins,' probably because the first ones they came across had painted their faces red for war. In any case, the moniker stood the test of time. Now we call 'em redskins, even though they ain't any such thing."

Captain Little was about to go on with his history lesson when two men appeared out of the gloom. They were a skinny, sorry-looking pair, Tyler observed, with tangled, umkempt hair and clothes that seemed poorly suited for the journey they were about to set out on. A sour, whiskey smell rose off them like steam, and the captain regarded them with a frown.

"In the dark last night you chaps didn't look too bad," he grumbled, "but in the morning light I can see you ain't nothin' but a couple wharf rats. My sniffer tells me you did more'n your share of farewellin' last night, too."

He waved them off. "On your way, boys! I got me a couple lively lads here who'll be able to work circles around you!"

Tyler felt sorry for the pair who shuffled off into the morning darkness. He knew exactly how they felt—just like he and Isaac had yesterday when they were rudely dismissed by the captain of the *Undaunted*.

After further prodding from Captain Little, the eight sleeping bodies scattered around the *Darlin' Nell* turned into men who stretched and yawned. The captain stuck a tin mug of hot coffee in the hand of each one.

None of them looked much livelier than the two who'd just left, but each seemed to know what to do after Captain Little loosed the chain that bound the keelboat to the wharf. When the current caught the *Darlin' Nell*, twisting her sideways in the river, each man grabbed a long pole, plunged it into the water, and turned the vessel nose-first against the current.

Tyler and Isaac exchanged no-turning-back glances. "I reckon we know now what the cap'n meant when he said powered by ever'thing but steam," Isaac muttered glumly. "Before we see Missouri again, Ty, you an' me are goin' to get the kind of exercise that'll make growin' hemp seem like a Sunday picnic."

Chapter Five

Tyler's heart stuck in his throat like a half-swallowed frog as the keelboat moved farther from shore. The stern-wheelers, the levee, the warehouses vanished in the fog, leaving the *Darlin' Nell* alone in the mist.

Sooner stood with his legs braced wide, accustoming himself to the movement of the boat. His ears were pricked forward, and his wolfish red muzzle was raised to test the strange new smells on the air. Tyler saw the dog's brown eye gleam with curiosity, while the blue one regarded the vessel and its occupants with detachment.

At that moment Captain Little leaned so close that Tyler felt warm, stale-tobacco breath dampen his cheek.

"Couldn't help notice that you packed a rifle on board this mornin', laddie," Captain Little murmured. His voice was pitched low so no one else could hear what he had to say. "If you don't mind some advice from an old man, you'd be wise to stash it inside the cargo box. Someone on board might take a notion to relieve you of it."

Tyler couldn't imagine anything worse than losing Elway's rifle before the trip had even started. "You mean just lean it inside the doorway?"

"Trust me, son, it'll be safe there," the captain assured him with a nod. Tyler went forward and rested the rifle inside the main opening of the hold.

"I been thinkin' about something else you said," the captain whispered after Tyler returned to stand at his side. "As I recall, you mentioned you had some money your stepdaddy gave you."

Tyler didn't answer. He gave Captain Little a wary glance. "Now son, don't look at me like it's *me* who might rob you," Captain Little protested. "I got to warn you about my crew, though. There's simply ain't no telling which one of these fellers has picked up some light-fingered habits as he traveled down the highway of life."

"I reckon I'd feel better hanging on to the money myself," Tyler hedged.

The captain shrugged lightly. "Suit yourself, lad. It'd be a shame, though, if one a them chaps picked your pocket while you slept. Wouldn't be the first time it'd been done, you know. Anyone ever tell you Dan'l Boone lost forty thousand dollars just that way? His pockets was picked as he snoozed, that's how."

Tyler bit his lip. If such a thing had happened to the likes of Dan'l Boone . . .

"You got a safe place to put it?" he asked. The thought of turning loose of the wages Elway had paid him made his knees weak.

"Indeed I do, son. Got a strongbox with a lock on it. I'm the only one with a key, which I keep on my person at all times."

It'd be terrible to get out to the territories without a penny because some rascal had picked your pocket, Tyler realized. He wouldn't have money to buy ammunition for Elway's rifle or anything else. "All right," he agreed. "Providing you give it right back as soon as we get where we're going," he said before the captain took it.

"Why, of course, laddie. I'm only looking out for your best interests, same as if you were my very own boy. Later, when the men are occupied, I'll put your money in the strongbox where it'll be safe as can be." The captain tucked the bills into the same pocket that held his tobacco. Then, after a moment's pause, he murmured, "And your friend, Isaac—he have any money?"

Uncle Matt always said that a smart man never put all his money in one bank. If one got robbed, a person would still have something left in the other one.

"No, sir, not a cent," Tyler said, surprised at how easily the lie came to his lips. "You know how black folks are. With money in their pockets they're apt to take off on you like scalded hogs," he added, using Isaac's very own words.

The captain chuckled. "I reckon that's true," he said.

"Only asked, mind you, because I figured I ought to protect his interests, too, you boys bein' so young and all."

As soon as they had a moment alone, Tyler vowed to tell Isaac to take the money out of his pocket, hide it in his shoe, and never mention that he had any.

Then Captain Little made an announcement to everyone aboard.

"We'll try to get upriver as far as Buffalo Point by sundown. That's where the river almost loops back on itself before it takes a northwesterly course again. We'll pull into a cove, out of the way of the steamers, and let 'em go by."

The captain climbed atop the cargo box and settled himself at the stern end. "You chaps better pray this fog lifts," he suggested, "because the Missouri can betray a man quicker'n a jealous woman."

Isaac took the captain at his word and bent his head to pray. Feeling foolish, Tyler did the same. He wished he knew a prayer that fit the occasion, but the only one that came to him was "Our Father." When he came to the "deliver us from evil" part, he sneaked a peek under his lashes and was amazed to see the misty shroud around the *Darlin' Nell* had begun to lift.

Captain Little took hold of a steering pole that was held in place by a Y-shaped wood fork attached to the stern end of the cargo box. Beneath his feet, Tyler felt the relentless current press the boat downriver. Without needing a direct order, each of the eight men—four on the right, or starboard, four on the left, or larboard—took up their poles again.

"*A bas les perches*—down with the poles!" bellowed Captain Little. At that command, each man thrust his pole into the river and pressed the narrower end, which was curved in a blunt, shoelike shape, against muddy bottom. Next, each man strode toward the stern of the *Darlin' Nell,* the larger, smooth end of the pole cradled in the hollow of his shoulder. Slowly, the boat was propelled against the current.

"*Levez les perches*—raise the poles!" Captain Little called. The men raised their poles and retreated quickly to the bow again, so as not to lose the forward momentum they'd gained. The process was repeated again and again. Punctuated by the captain's cries, the *Darlin' Nell* moved laboriously upstream.

"Pole and push, push and pole—that's one of the ways a keelboat makes its way against the current," Captain Little explained. "I'd have had me a steamer long ago if I could've afforded one. On the other hand, *Nell* has certain advantages. No need to stoke her engine full of wood or coal, because what powers her is good, old-fashioned elbow grease."

"Din't I tell you, Ty?" Isaac whispered. "Ever'thing but steam means muscle power. I reckon I could write you a book about what *that* means!"

"Hold out your arms," Captain Little ordered abruptly. "Let me see if you boys got enough length on you to do a proper job of poling." He examined them shrewdly from under the brim of his soiled cap. "Yep, I think you both got a reach that'll do. Within the hour, you can spell two of the others. Then, after you rest awhile, you can spell two more. That way, nobody'll get too wore out."

Using his pipe as a pointer, the captain directed Tyler's and Isaac's attention to the walkway, a scant yard wide on either side of the boat, where the men walked back and forth. Wooden cleats were nailed about thirty inches apart, the distance of a man's stride, the entire length of each walkway from stern to bow.

"French voyageurs called it the *passe avant*, or 'pass before,' and you can plainly see the purpose of those cleats," he said. "Gives a man something to brace his feet against as he presses forward with his pole. Otherwise, he might lose his footing, especially when the deck gets slick with rain or sleet."

The *Darlin' Nell* created no wake as she was poled along, then as the fog lightened further, Captain Little suddenly cried out in dismay.

"Look out—a dead man to starboard!" he yelled, his voice shrill. Tyler and Isaac whirled to stare. Forty feet to the right they could plainly see the dark, curved back of someone lying in the water. It was a drowned man, sure enough, floating along facedown.

"How'd he die?" Tyler whispered, remembering the sight of skeletons stacked like cordwood in the cemetery at Pea Ridge when he'd gone off to look for Papa.

"Phsaw!" Captain Little snorted. "That ain't a *man!* In river lingo, a dead man's a dead tree. Some folks call 'em sawyers. Don't matter what you call 'em, though, it means a tree that's been uprooted upstream. Dead men are the reason we'll never travel at night unless the moon's extra bright."

"*Levez les perches!*" Captain Little called to the men who were poling. The instant the poles were raised, he expertly steered the *Darlin' Nell* larboard, away from danger.

"Dead men ain't the only hazard the Missouri's got waitin' for us," he warned. "Sandbars can ground a boat quick as a wink. Shallows where none are expected will do the same. Worse, dead men lurking below the surface can reach up and bust your keel." He sighed, reflecting on the hard life of an old boatman who couldn't afford a steamship.

"Just the same, we'll try to make good time every day, on account of the river will be froze solid as a piece of sheet iron come December. If we had runners, *Nell* could skate upriver then!" He grinned at his own pleasantry. "But we don't, so it behooves us to make haste before the weather forces us to make a winter camp."

Tyler coughed politely. He liked the captain's use of *we.* Even though one or more of the men might be light-fingered, it sounded as if everyone—he and Isaac included—were in this adventure together.

"Make a winter camp?" Tyler repeated. How could the eight men who were poling—plus the captain and Isaac and himself, eleven souls in all, not counting Sooner—live through the winter huddled cheek by jowl in the narrow cargo box of the *Darlin' Nell?*

"Why, we'll go ashore and cobble together a suitable shelter," the captain said, as if he understood what was on Tyler's mind. "There's lots of trees up and down the Missouri, willows and cottonwoods and aspen by the score. Then once we get a roof over our heads we'll settle down to trade."

"How'll the Indians know we're there?"

"I can see you don't know much about Indians, my boy. They got ways of knowing things even before a fella knows they know 'em," Richard Little declared. "They post scouts hither and thither, or have runners, or some such. In any case, they'll know we've arrived before we see hide or hair of 'em. Soon as they're sure our intentions are peaceful, they'll start to come around."

The sun tinted the rising fog shades of pale pink and peach. Trees and bushes along the distant shore slid by like ghosts. No signs of civilization could be seen, and Tyler realized St. Joseph already was far behind. His heart gave a quirky thonk against his breastbone. Sooner, however, had moved to the bow and gave no sign he cared a whit about leaving St. Joe or civilization.

"All right, lads, time for you to take a turn at poling," Captain Little announced, rousing Tyler from his brief attack of homesickness. "You and Isaac relieve these two fellers here." In spite of the coolness of the morning, the faces of the two men who gave up their poles were as shiny with sweat as if they'd been buttered.

"Follow the rhythm of the man in front of you," the captain directed. "Move forward as he moves forward. Turn lively on your heel when you get all the way to the stern and start the exercise all over again."

Tyler went starboard; Isaac went larboard. Tyler tried to imitate the action of the man ahead of him but found it hard to do. His first attempt to dip his pole smoothly into the water, lean hard against it, and press forward was clumsy.

"Like I said, sonny, get a rhythm!" Captain Little barked impatiently. "Otherwise you'll be as much good to me as a three-legged horse!"

It wasn't long before Tyler felt perspiration trickle down the ladder of his ribs, soaking his shirt through. On the far side of the cargo box, he heard Isaac grunt with effort. Pole in; press to the river bottom; step forward; retreat to the bow. Do it again, head down, hunched over like a mule in harness. Tyler soon was hypnotized by the repetition of his labor.

To Captain Little's delight, a light wind came up at noon. "Drop an anchor," he ordered. "We've got a wind at our backs, so let's hoist some sail." Within moments, the men had set a mast, which was already rigged and lay to one side of the cargo box. They ran up a large, once-white square of canvas and a small jib sheet. The moment the sails filled with wind and the anchor was lifted, *Darlin' Nell* scooted upstream.

"We'll savor our luck while it lasts, because we won't get a breeze like this every day," the captain lamented. "Or if we do it'll blow agin us from the north." Then he cocked his head at Isaac.

"Ain't you the one who bragged you boys knew how to cook?" he reminded him. "How about rustling up some vittles for these men here?"

Tyler saw Isaac turn pale beneath his dark skin. "V-V-Vittles?" he stammered.

"It's part of our bargain, remember? I said I'd treat you right and in turn you'd treat me right." The captain pointed to the cargo box. "I got stuff in there that'll last us for a time—spuds, onions, beans, salt pork, hardtack, and such like. Go fetch something and cook up whatever strikes your fancy."

But as Isaac trotted down the *passe avant* toward the entry of the cargo box, Captain Little caught him by the sleeve.

"One thing both you boys got to remember," he said, his cheery voice suddenly stern. "The only time—*only time*, mind you—that you got permission to go into the hold is to fetch vittles, hear? Nobody is allowed in there unless I go with him, understand? That way, I don't have to worry about my inventory ending up in someone else's possession."

Isaac nodded, and continued down the pass. "And you, son," he told Tyler, his voice resuming its cheeriness, "you stoke up this here little cookstove so your friend can tantalize our taste buds with a delectable concoction. You'll find a few sticks of wood beside it, and we'll get more tonight when we tie up and wait for the steamers to go by."

What Isaac concocted was plain fare—boiled potatoes, onions, and a small chunk of salt pork for each man. Served hot, it didn't taste too bad. Tyler expected loud complaints, but the men ate silently, like a crew of mutes. It wasn't Captain Little's nature to remain quiet for long, however.

"Why, I haven't minded my manners," he said, forking a chunk of potato into his mouth. "I ain't introduced you boys to the crew, or them to you." He drummed his spoon against the edge of his tin plate.

"Gentlemen, these here lads are Isaac—he's the dark one and Tyler's the pale one—who claim to be from Sweet Creek, Missouri." Three men nodded a sullen greeting. The others kept their eyes fastened on their food, shoveling it into their mouths as if they were stoking furnaces.

"Going from stern to bow, boys—first names only, because it's all that matters among us—there's Bodie and Pierre, who've made this trip with me before. Next comes Henry, Luther, then Billy and James, who are brothers. Those two chaps far to the bow are Johnny and

Warner, a pair of good ol' river rats I've known for many a day."

Tyler did his best to fix each man's name in his mind. After all, these strangers were family now.

As Captain Little predicted, the wind turned quirky. It puffed up to move the vessel too fast to avoid dead men, or died off to let *Darlin' Nell* be tugged backward by the current. Yet the river was too deep to pole, so the captain put another method of locomotion into action.

"Time for the oars, men," Captain Little said. "Drop the sail and we'll take up oars for a time." From inside the cargo box he produced eight oars, and grumbling, each man took one.

"Too early in the trip to be bellyachin'," he warned, a steely sound in his voice. "We ain't but a day outta St. Joe, and you ain't even had to do any cordelling yet!"

As before, Tyler and Isaac spelled the other men. The afternoon wore on. Tyler's shoulders burned with pain. He wore blisters on each hand, and wondered if walking to the territories might've have been easier.

Then he noticed how Isaac worked: patiently, eyes half-closed, his face naked of expression. Maybe that's what he learned when he was a slave to some master, Tyler mused as he shut his own eyes and pulled against the current. Me, I could always find a way to go off to fish for an hour, or lie in the cool, dark barn on hot summer days. But I was white, and nobody's slave. Isaac was black; for him, it had always been different.

Tyler was never so glad in his life to see the sun start to go down. As it descended toward the west, Captain Little spied a likely place to tie up for the night. "Let's point *Nell's* nose over there, boys," he said, indicating a cluster of willow and cottonwood that grew along the edge of an island in the middle of the river.

The rusty chain that had held *Darlin' Nell* to the levee in St. Joe was retrieved. Once the boat got close to shore, the man named Billy leaped off and looped the chain around the trunk of a stout tree.

The narrow strip of sandy beach surrounding the island was littered with driftwood. "Stack some of that up," the captain directed, "and we'll start a good fire." Then he drew Tyler aside.

"Laddie, go fetch your rifle from the cargo box," he murmured. "There's still some good light left in the sky, so take a walk into those woods behind me and see if you can rustle up some fresh meat for supper."

The only thing Tyler had ever shot in his life was a young buck just before Christmas a year ago. With no meat in the house, he'd had no choice, yet he'd always regretted the surprised look in the animal's eyes as the bullet struck it and blood had blossomed in the snow like fallen roses.

"Got no choice this time, either," he reminded himself,

and struck off into the thick brush that covered the middle of the island. He hoped he wouldn't come across anything big—a bear, or a wildcat.

He stepped lightly through the damp leaves. Behind him, the voices of the men who were gathering wood grew fainter and fainter. Then, in a small gloaming, he came on a young buck, its new antlers no more than nubbins on its crown. The animal raised its head and stared at him, curious and unafraid.

Probably never saw a human before, Tyler realized, and fired before the creature could bound away. Unlike the deer he'd killed back home and had to track a mile through deep snow, this one dropped in its tracks. It trembled once, then was still. Tyler opened its jugular with his pocketknife so it could bleed properly. He'd need help dragging it back to the beach, though, so he retraced his steps.

"I got you some meat all right," he told Captain Little, "but I reckon I'll need help getting it back here."

The captain beckoned to the man named Henry. "Henry's got the back of an ox," he said genially. "He'll give you a hand."

Henry did more than give a hand. When they got to the spot where the buck lay, its shiny eyes dulled, Henry seized it by the hind legs and hoisted it over his shoulder. As he strode toward camp, Tyler saw the last drops of the deer's life splatter brightly on the back of Henry's boots.

"But I don't reckon you aim to eat this critter

tonight," he told Captain Little. "Papa always said new-killed meat should be left to season a few days before it was butchered."

Captain Little laughed and clamped an affectionate hand on Tyler's shoulder. "With all due respect to your daddy, son, we're goin' to eat this venison the way red folks do, still warm with life and hardly cooked a-tall."

He directed the man named Pierre to gut the animal and skin it. The liver was tossed to Sooner, so hot that it steamed in the cooling air. Chunks were sliced off the haunch, then each man cut himself a willow stick and commenced to roast his own portion over the fire.

Tyler ate with a queasy stomach. The mild astonishment in the buck's eyes was so fresh in his mind, he couldn't enjoy his meal. Isaac had no such qualms. He scarfed down his share with a lusty appetite, licking up the scarlet juices as they dripped off his chin.

The sandy beach still held the heat of the September sun when Tyler gratefully stretched himself out. The coals of the dying fire cast a rosy glow in all directions, and the familiar fragrance of Captain Little's evening pipe floated on the air.

"Isaac?" Tyler called sleepily. "You as tired as me?" The only answer from Isaac was a wuffle. Beside him, Sooner adjusted his bones and heaved a contented sigh, his belly full of liver and hard as a drum. On the far side of the fire, Tyler heard Captain Little knock out his pipe and settle himself for sleep.

Tyler raised himself on one elbow. A few feet away, the river was sprinkled with stars as it slid past the island. The sliver of a new moon hung low in the west, reminding Tyler of his trip to Texas to find Papa.

I'm far from home again, he thought with a touch of astonishment. Except this time he wasn't looking for Papa. This time, he was looking for Tyler Bohannon, a boy who'd lost his place at home and needed to find a new one.

CHAPTER SIX

By the first week of October, Captain Little announced they'd made better time than he'd hoped for. "You been a mighty fine crew," he told everyone, seizing each man's hand for a hearty shake, including Tyler's and Isaac's.

"And when we get up yonder to Fort Benton, there'll be a bonus for those who hired on," he promised. Tyler wondered if he and Isaac—though Captain Little had made it clear they wouldn't be paid a wage—also might get a dollar or two.

"A bonus?" Bodie growled. "Fort Benton's a mighty long ways off, Cap'n. Meantime, can't we have a little oil to grease our rusty hinges?"

"Ah, Bodie! Don't take up your old troublemakin' ways again," the captain cautioned. "You been upriver with me before, and know full well I run a tight ship. If you aim to get that bonus I just mentioned, you'll do things *my* way."

Tyler glanced at Captain Little in surprise. The old man's voice was as sharp as a freshly honed knife, and the steely look he gave Bodie made the other man lower his sullen gaze. Tyler wondered what kind of grease Bodie had in mind, and how he planned to use it.

After their first day on the river, Tyler and Isaac didn't need to be reminded it was their job to cook, but Isaac soon willingly turned most of it over to Tyler.

Each evening as soon as the *Darlin' Nell* was secured and a fire had been built on shore, Tyler set a pot of river water to boil while Isaac peeled potatoes and carrots. Tyler dropped them into the pot, imitating as best he could what he'd seen Mama do at home. Next, he added onions and chunks of meat he carved off whatever critter he'd been lucky enough to shoot. He used salt sparingly, because Captain Little warned their supply had to last the whole trip.

Even though the weather had cooled, blowflies were still a plague, which meant fresh venison lasted hardly a week before it turned green and maggoty. If Tyler only got a woodchuck or a couple rabbits after they tied up, those were eaten up quick, which meant he had to hunt more often. With a few well-timed sighs, he registered his aggravation at having to ask permission each time he needed to retrieve Elway's Winchester from the cargo box.

"Ah, son, I get the meanin' of those groans," Captain Little said with a smile. "Mind you, it ain't that I don't trust you a heap. But if those other fellers see you traipsing back and forth like you owned what's in there, they'll be tempted to take liberties themselves," he explained, the ever-present wreath of pipe smoke swirling about his head.

"First thing you know, I'd be missin' some of the wares I aim to trade with the *peaux rouges*. Can't have that, now can I?" He massaged Tyler's shoulder with a friendly paw. "So even though you think I'm an old fuss-budget, hew to my rules, and no one will entertain any notions of thievery."

The aroma of a bubbling stew or roasting meat was always enough to bring the men close to the fire each evening. They hunkered down, their squabbles from earlier in the day put aside—except for Bodie, who was quarrelsome from sunup to sundown. But when the thin-as-a-whip man named John brought out his harmonica and played a few lonesome tunes, even Bodie was lulled into a mellow mood.

Such evenings made Tyler understand why Papa got so attached to the men in his command. Maybe it was part of what lured him across the Texas border into Mexico. He'd traded a wife, two sons, and a daughter for the company of strangers, for nights around a campfire and sleeping under a star-pocked sky. Tyler felt a twinge of guilt. Such company might keep him away from home a long time, too.

"I reckon the last few breaths of that warm Gulf air might push us up almost to Fort Pierre by the middle of the month," Captain Little declared one evening after venison stew had been ladled onto each man's tin plate. "Good thing, too, because this uncommonly fine weather ain't goin' to last forever."

After supper, each man rinsed his plate and spoon in the river so they'd be ready for the morning meal. Breakfast would be another serving of stew, because Tyler had learned to cook enough for more than one meal at a time. If the captain were eager to be gone in the morning, however, the stew would be served cold, a pale sheet of grease congealed on its surface.

One by one, the men rolled themselves into their blankets. Captain Little filled his pipe and squatted by the fire as was his habit every evening. The sinking blaze made his cheeks rosier than ever, and the tip of his bulbous nose gleamed like a cherry.

Tyler smiled sleepily to himself. He'd become fond of the pudgy little chap, so quick to make a joke, to guffaw, and slap his knee, or to lay a comradely hand on a person's shoulder. You'd have to be made of stone not to like such a fellow.

For the first time since the trip began, Isaac took forever getting settled. The fuss he made even disturbed Sooner, who whined each time Isaac flopped from right side to left, then back again.

"You awake, Ty?" Isaac whispered after Captain Little had finished the ritual of knocking ashes from his pipe before rolling himself in his blanket.

"How could I be anything else with you flopping and flapping around like beached blue gill? Lie still, for lordy sakes," he hissed. "Your antics are giving Sooner fits, too!"

Isaac elbowed his way closer to Tyler. He lowered his voice till it was so soft it was hard to make out his words. "Ty, what's *contraband* mean?" His breath was warm against the back of Tyler's neck.

"Where'd you ever hear a word like that?" Tyler grunted.

"You heard it same time I did," Isaac reminded him.

"I did?" Tyler tried to recollect, but was too sleepy to fix his thoughts on when it might have been.

"Sure enough. The captain of the *Undaunted* told us he didn't carry any contraband, remember?"

Tyler frowned in the dark. He searched his mind for what the word might mean. Once, Mr. Blackburn said that *contradiction* meant something was in opposition to something else. He said the *contra* part came from a Latin word that meant "against." If you saw it in an everyday word like *contrary*, you could be pretty sure it meant one thing went against another thing.

"Maybe it means people aren't supposed to ship certain stuff up the Missouri," Tyler murmured. "Maybe it's all right for Captain Little to carry pots and pans but he's not supposed to haul other stuff."

"What other stuff?"

"How'm I supposed to know? I'm no expert on contraband."

Isaac fell silent. "Well, I think I saw some of it—that contraband stuff—amongst what Captain Little's got aboard the *Darlin' Nell.*"

Suddenly Tyler was wide awake. He rolled over so his nose almost touched Isaac's. It would be best if their words didn't drift into other ears.

"Saw it tonight," Isaac said. "When I went into the cargo box to get you them spuds for supper."

"How could you tell it was contraband?" Tyler wasn't sure he'd recognize any, even in broad daylight. The inside of that cargo box was dark and gloomy, so how could Isaac be sure—

"There was only a few spuds left in that sack next to the door, so I went lookin' for more," Isaac explained. "At the back of the hold, I came acrost a barrel. It was leakin' a little, so I stopped to check. I figured it might be mo'lassus—mo'lassus come in barrels, you know— if it was, we could cook us some good beans or pour it over our biscuits. Everybody gettin' mighty tired of eatin' stew practically ever' single night." Isaac paused. "Except there weren't mo'lassus in that barrel."

"How could you tell?"

"How d'you think? I took me a taste!" Isaac blurted, then clapped his hand over his mouth. "Mo'lassus be sweet and thick," he said, lowering his voice. "This stuff be sour—I mean, *real* sour—thin as water, too. It burned a hot trail clear down to my belly button."

"Was it . . . whiskey?"

Tyler remembered taking a swallow from a jug Papa kept stashed in the root cellar, just to see if he could figure out why Papa liked it so much and Mama hated it so bad. He'd darn near strangled, and never tried a second draft.

"You bet your sweet life it was," Isaac whispered.

"Maybe Captain Little keeps it in case the men get sick," Tyler said. When Papa came down with the flu the winter before he went to war, it made him feel better to have a toddy—a steaming mug of hot water, whiskey, and sugar all stirred together. At such times, Mama didn't scold him. She even made the toddy herself, then carried it to where Papa languished in the big iron bed they shared in the room behind the kitchen.

"A whole barrel in case the men get sick?" Isaac grumbled. "I reckon you got more faith in Cap'n Little than I do."

"You got him figured wrong," Tyler objected. Only a moment ago he'd been thinking how much he liked the cheery old man. Isaac's problem was he'd been treated so bad in his other life that he was even suspicious of someone as jolly as St. Nicholas.

"You ain't come up like I have," Isaac reminded Tyler, as if reflecting on his past, too. "Isaac learned a long time ago how to spot a man wit' a hard heart."

A hard heart? It rankled Tyler to hear Captain Little talked about that way. The man's heart was soft as his handshake! Besides, hadn't Sooner taken to him right off?

"What gives you such a notion?" Tyler demanded. He reckoned he could read a man as well as Isaac Peerce any old day of the week. If Captain Little were wicked, he'd be the first to guess it.

"It's this feelin' I got," Isaac murmured. "Isaac learned a long time ago to trust what he feels way deep down in his bowels. Can't explain it no better'n that, Ty."

When Isaac fell silent, Tyler let his thoughts drift back to the captain of the *Undaunted*. Exactly what had he said that evening in St. Joe?

"I don't carry contraband on my ship as is the habit of some vessels you might find docked at this levee," were his very words. Except he didn't say which vessels he had in mind.

Tyler tried to puzzle it out. Number one, if the captain of the *Undaunted* knew certain things were illegal, and number two, if Captain Little hid the whiskey toward the back of the cargo box as Isaac claimed, then number three, Captain Little probably also knew such things were against the law.

"Keep your lip buttoned about this," Tyler whispered against Isaac's cheek. No way would he take Isaac's word for this. First chance he got, he'd find an excuse to go into the cargo box himself.

● ● ●

Tyler waited patiently for a good reason to ask Captain Little's permission to go inside the hold. To sneak in there on the sly would only create more trouble. But there was plenty of fresh meat on hand and no reason to make another stew. When no excuse presented itself to fetch potatoes or carrots, Tyler contented himself with studying the captain for signs of wickedness where he hadn't seen any before.

Each day Captain Little was as pink and cheerful as the day before. He often hummed a merry tune under his breath, usually "Turkey in the Straw" or "Sweet Betsy from Pike," a good-natured lilt in his voice and his twinkly blue eyes as full of easeful humor as always.

Even men as sour as Bodie and Pierre sometimes smiled at his jokes. "A person don't need a cup to get a drink from the Big Muddy," he said one day, "a spoon and fork works better." He joshed that the Missouri was too thick to drink but too thin to plow.

But after Isaac's accident, the routine aboard the *Darlin' Nell* changed. He had been helping Pierre take down the sails when he caught his fingers in the socket that the mast fit into. He didn't holler, but when he held up his mashed thumb and index finger they looked like stubs of raw venison. Captain Little clucked with sympathy, wrapped Isaac's fingers in a piece of torn cloth, then turned to Tyler.

"The light's getting so dim, we might run into a dead man if we try to make it to shore tonight," he announced, "so we'll drop anchor and stay right where we are. Supper will have to be all your doing, son, on account of this boy here ain't goin' to be peelin' spuds or anything else till he heals up some."

"Well, sir, we don't have enough meat left to boil up a piece for each man, but Isaac's the only one who's got permission to fetch spuds and onions to make stew," Tyler said. "Is it all right if I go into the cargo box to get 'em?"

"Granted—but mind I ain't givin' you blanket permission," Captain Little answered sharply. "Ask *each* time you need something in there, hear?"

"Yes, sir, on my word," Tyler promised.

The only light coming into the hold through the small square windows along either side grew fainter as evening deepened. Tyler located a fresh sack of potatoes and another of carrots only three feet from the door, counted out two for each man plus a couple for Sooner, and dropped them in a tin bucket. He spied the barrel Isaac mentioned. He bent and took a quick sniff.

Whiskey, sure enough.

Nearby were wooden boxes labeled BEADS in clumsy white letters. Next to them were crates marked CLOTH. Swiftly, Tyler peered into each one. They were filled with beads and cloth. He breathed a sigh of relief. So much for what Isaac's bowels had told him.

At the back of the hold were other boxes. One of them was labeled SCISSORS, NEEDLES, AWLS. Tyler hastily opened one. In the faint light he saw the gleam of metal. He looked closer.

Weren't scissors and needles usually silver colored? His heart hammered as he stared at row after neat row of brass cartridge casings. He checked a second box. More ammunition. He was about to check a third but knew he'd already lingered too long. He grabbed two onions, and was careful to paste a noncommittal expression on his face as he stepped onto the *passe avant*.

"Can't talk now," Tyler whispered to Isaac as he started a fire in Captain Little's washtub contraption on the top of the cargo box. He proceeded to peel vegetables and keep his expression ordinary. "But I reckon your hunch was right."

The men hated the idea of staying on board all night. It made John so crabby he refused to play any lonesome tunes on his harmonica. Supper—another despised stew—was eaten peevishly, after which the men didn't lean over the side of the *Darlin' Nell* to rinse their plates. They flopped down, their backs pressed against the cargo box on either starboard or larboard side, the better to soak up what little warmth from the sun had been stored there during the day.

"So you find that barrel I tol' you about?" Isaac asked as he stretched out next to Tyler at the bow with Sooner curled in between.

"Whiskey's the least of what's in there," Tyler said.

"What you mean?"

"Did you see those boxes marked 'Beads' and 'Cloth'?"

"Ty, you know full well Isaac can only read a few words—and beads or cloth ain't two of 'em."

"Well, some of 'em are full of cartridges. Look just like the ones Mr. Snepp gave me for the Winchester. There's gotta be hundreds of 'em, enough to start a war."

"Cartridges?" Isaac echoed. "If there's cartridges, then there's gotta be—"

"Yep. The captain must have rifles, too."

"What we goin' to do?" Isaac whispered, cradling his damaged fingers against his breastbone as if the news made them hurt worse.

"Do? We ain't going to do anything," Tyler said. "Not yet. This is something I got to ponder awhile." The problem was, where could they run to? They hadn't arrived at Fort Pierre yet, and the land beyond the banks on either side of the river were wild, bleak, and empty.

After a breakfast of oatmeal (Tyler took care to pick out the weevils before he boiled it up), Captain Little decided there was time to gather fresh kindling for the firebox. "You lads take the skiff and nip ashore to get some," he suggested. He clapped Isaac on the shoulder in a grandfatherly fashion. "And to make it easy on them fingers, boy, you let Tyler do all the rowing and chopping while you load the skiff one-handed."

Neither boy spoke as Tyler rowed toward the shore.

When they dragged the skiff a few feet onto the beach, Isaac whispered, "So you done some ponderin', Ty?"

Tyler let the ax dangle from his hand. "Nobody can hear us now," he said, "so we don't need to whisper." He squinted toward the *Darlin' Nell,* anchored a hundred yards away. The captain was at his usual post at the stern, his gaze trained on the shore. Tyler busied himself with chopping driftwood into proper lengths. No sense giving the old man reason to be suspicious.

"Why do you suppose Captain Little fibbed to us, Isaac?" he asked between ax blows. "Why'd he tell us he was going to trade pots and pans and bangles and beads if all along he aimed to trade rifles and ammunition? And what's the whiskey for?"

"You know how folks get when they drink it," Isaac pointed out. "Foolish. Easy. They do things they wouldn't do if their heads was clear."

Tyler remembered how merry Papa was when he came back from town, smelling sweetly from what he'd drunk at the tavern in New Hope. He was so good-natured he never minded that Mama hollered and wagged her finger under his nose. Whiskey probably did the same thing to everyone. Did that mean when the captain traded with them he intended to give the red men a few pulls off a jug, to make it easier to cut deals for furs and robes?

"Whiskey's bad enough, Isaac," Tyler murmured. "It's those rifles and cartridges that fret me most. If they're really contraband, and if the government finds out what the captain's up to—" He paused, and squinted toward where the *Darlin' Nell* rocked on the river.

"What would happen to *us* if the government catches Captain Little? Maybe we'd get arrested, too. We'd never have a chance to get where we want to go."

Tyler wished he could take back his former fondness for the captain. The man whose jokes had been so agreeable wasn't what he seemed to be. Captain Little was no St. Nicholas. Tyler moistened his lips. The next words that tumbled out of his mouth were ones he never expected to hear.

"First chance we get, Isaac, you and me better figure out a way to cut loose from the captain."

CHAPTER SEVEN

"Cut loose from 'im?" Isaac said with a snort. "And do what?" Disgust filled his dark eyes. "Ty Bohannon, ain't no way for us to get up this muddy ol' river if we don't do it on the *Darlin' Nell*. Truth is, we is prisoners same's if we was in chains."

"Horses—we could get us a couple horses," Tyler suggested weakly.

"Horses?" Isaac scanned the horizon under a visor made of his bandaged hand. "I shore don't see no horses out there. If you know where you goin' to get some, you ain't told Isaac about it."

"Shoot! I know they're not just wandering around, bridled and saddled and waiting for us to climb aboard!" Tyler snapped. "But there's settlers around here some-where, Isaac. That's what Mr. Lincoln's Homestead Act was all about—opening up the West for homesteaders.

Such folks probably got horses—and we got money, right? We could buy one for you and one for me."

Isaac searched the horizon again. "Don't see no settlers out there neither," he observed drily.

"Quit!" Tyler exclaimed, whacking at a dead tree branch. "The point is, Isaac, we got to figure out how to get away from Captain Little as quick as we can. If trading arms is against the law, sooner or later the law will catch up with him. If we stick around, we might end up in the same kettle of stew the captain does."

Tyler paused as his glance fell on the skiff, half-loaded with wood, which was pulled up at the river's edge.

"Maybe we don't need horses, Isaac," he said slowly. "We got that skiff. . . . The next time the captain sends us ashore, we won't go back. We'll head downstream till we find a cove to tie up in. . . . The captain won't take time to hunt for us on account of he's hellbent on making good time in the other direction."

Isaac looked at Tyler as if he pitied his dimwittedness. "How you figger to make progress agin the kind of current we been fightin' for weeks, Ty? You seen what a mighty struggle it be for the *Darlin' Nell*—with a crew of ten if you count you and me—not to mention poles, oars, a sail, and rope enough to cordelle 'er to kingdom come. Besides, what happens when winter comes? We got no supplies, we got no—"

"We got no time to argue, either," Tyler broke in.

Every point Isaac made was as sharp as a knife blade. No way could they move a flimsy, eight-foot skiff upriver against the relentless flow of the Missouri. "We got other things to worry about right now, like getting this wood back before Captain Little wonders what's taking us so long."

The next afternoon, Captain Little steered the *Darlin' Nell* into exactly the kind of snug cove Tyler imagined he and Isaac could hide in if they escaped downstream. Almost-bare cottonwoods grew close to shore, their fallen leaves glowing as brightly as lemons in the shallow water. A sandy beach curved invitingly in the shape of a crescent moon. Beyond, a low bluff to the northwest offered protection from the wind. A long sandbar prevented *Darlin' Nell* from being pulled up close, so the captain ordered the anchor dropped and the skiff lowered to take everyone ashore two or three at a time.

"We'll settle here for a spell," the captain announced. There was a note of glee in his voice. "And it won't surprise me a particle if some a them red folks happened along. I've stopped at this very spot before, and they know I show up about the same time every year." He gave Tyler a wink, the sort a grandfather might give a favorite grandson. This time, Tyler could manage only a feeble smile in reply.

"While we wait, Tyler can pick us off another deer and we'll have some fresh-roasted meat instead of another infernal stew," the captain teased in his usual merry way. It was as if he wanted to make it up to the crew for sleeping overnight on the *Darlin' Nell.*

What if Isaac and me are wrong about him? Tyler asked himself, stricken by sudden doubt. Maybe the captain could explain about the whiskey, the cartridges, the guns. Just the same, he signaled Isaac with a glance: Soon as we eat, before those Indians show up, let's take our chances, cut out of here, and hope for the best.

"If the boy gets some meat, I'd sure appreciate a glass of whiskey to wash it down," Bodie growled.

Tyler grimaced. To Bodie, he'd always been *the boy,* never a boy with a name. As he hefted Elway's rifle in the crook of his arm, Tyler peeked at Captain Little to see if the mention of whiskey stirred a response, but he paid Bodie no mind at all.

Toward late afternoon, Tyler helped Pierre skin and gut a doe he'd shot as she had approached the river for a drink. She had a half-grown fawn with her, which made him loathe to take her life. He was worried enough about his own, however, that he hardened his heart and felled her with a clean shot.

As before, each man carved a chunk off the haunch and set himself to roasting it over the fire. Tyler was about to take his third chaw of charred, juicy venison when Captain Little gave a loud guffaw. He pointed to the top of the bluff.

Indians—twenty or more of them—sat their mounts

in silence, the wind moving the manes of their ponies and stirring the feathers in their hair. They offered no greeting and made no move to come closer.

"Indians! You ever seen one before?" Isaac mumbled around a mouthful of meat, his dark eyes round as marbles.

"Nope," Tyler admitted, licking his fingers. Their silhouettes, savage against the hard blue sky, caused the fine hairs on the back of his neck to stand straight up. He'd been hungry, but to save himself he couldn't swallow another mouthful.

Captain Little, however, was elated. "What'd I tell you, boys?" He chuckled with a broad grin. He made a swipe at the meat drippings in his beard and cleaned his fingers on the seat of his trousers. "They've brought a couple extra ponies along to carry home the stuff they trade for. And long experience has taught me it helps to grease the wheels of commerce a bit."

The captain returned Tyler's startled glance with a sly smile. "Now son, don't look at me as nervous as a cat in a roomful of rockers," he murmured, laughing softly. "Means those red folks need to loosen up a little before we start doin' business. Makes it easier to drive a good bargain." He motioned to Isaac.

"Isaac, take the skiff out to the *Darlin' Nell* and drain off a half gallon from that leaky barrel at the back of the hold." Tyler saw Isaac nearly swallow his Adam's apple.

"Me, sir? You w-w-wants me t-t-to—"

"It's the grease of commerce, lad. In a word, whiskey. Most Indians crave the taste of it, which is why the gov'mint don't want folks like me to give 'em any. It tends to make red men rowdy, though, so only drain off enough to put 'em in a fine negotiating frame of mind but not enough to get 'em soused."

"Tell the darky to drain off a whole gallon while he's at it," Bodie demanded. "Like I said, me an' the others wouldn't mind a snort ourselves." Only two of the men—the brothers Billy and James—nodded in agreement.

In a flash, Tyler saw the captain's eyes narrow. "It's your job to keep a clear head about you, my good man," he warned. "We're here to trade, not take part in any festivities." Bodie sullenly inspected his chunk of dripping meat and fell silent.

"Henry and John, you chaps go back with Isaac and help load some beads and cloth and pots on the skiff, then stay behind to mind the vessel. I don't want any Indians swimmin' out there to help themselves," the captain ordered. He bent close and whispered in Tyler's ear.

"Iron Shell's got a hot head," he confided, "and there are certain items on the *Nell* that I don't want him to lay hands on. If he did, all hell might break loose." Tyler was sure the old man was referring to the contraband marked SCISSORS, NEEDLES, AWLS.

As Henry and John got ready to push off with the skiff, the captain called out, "Best you take Tyler's rifle with you, and the pooch, too. Red folks think there's nothin' tastier 'n dawg stew, and we don't want Sooner to end up in a pot, do we?"

Tyler gulped as he watched the Indians ride single file down the side of the bluff. They assembled themselves in a crescent-shaped gathering that imitated the shape of the cove itself. He glanced over his shoulder. Sooner, his red coat like a beacon, was already aboard the *Darlin' Nell,* standing safely at his mascot's post on the bow.

The Indians murmured among themselves, giving no indication they recognized Captain Little. When Isaac carried the jug up the beach, the captain set it down in the sand and beckoned the Indians to come forward. He called out in a language Tyler didn't understand, but the tall red man in the lead held up his palm and shook his head.

"Name's Maza Tanpeska, or Iron Shell," the captain confided under his breath. "He's the chief of a small band of Sioux, about twenty or thirty families. I remember the durn fool from other trades. Except he ain't a fool," he corrected himself.

"He claims whiskey makes men act foolish, which of course is its purpose. Well, ain't no sense antagonizing him. He's none too fond of whites, you see. Says we chop down too many trees along the river and scare the buffalo away. He's a hard bargainer, but usually good for a few pelts and maybe a robe or two."

Iron Shell didn't look like Tyler imagined an Indian chief would. He wore deerskin leggings and breech clout, sure enough, but his shirt was the kind a white man might wear—red and black plaid—and his blue jacket was decorated with a tattered yellow cavalry insignia. Taken from a dead soldier? Tyler wondered uneasily.

He felt Isaac's elbow in his ribs, and turned to look in the direction Isaac was pointing. Bodie had picked up the jug of whiskey and was taking several long, greedy swallows.

"Should I tell the cap'n?" Isaac whispered.

Bodie took three more long swigs, then set the jug down and corked it. "Keep still," Tyler advised. "I reckon he got what he wanted."

With a combination of words and sign language, Iron Shell indicated he wanted to see pots and pans and bolts of cloth.

"You, Isaac," the captain called, "go fetch what the chief wants from the skiff."

Isaac was on his feet in a second and returned with the goods. Iron Shell inspected the pots by holding them up to the light to make sure there were no holes in the bottoms. Next, he examined the cloth, fingering it like an expert. He picked out a bolt of blue and one of red, each patterned with small white flowers. He sorted through the beads and took three or four fistfuls, which he dropped into the empty pots. Next, each of the other Indian men made their own selections.

Then, out of the corner of his eye, Tyler saw Bodie uncork the whiskey jug again and take two more thirsty swigs.

In return for the pots and fabric and beads, Iron Shell directed one of his men to bring up several pelts. A pile of beaver, mink, and otter furs, plus a single fine, blue-gray fox pelt, were presented to Captain Little. After the captain made his selection (he picked the fox pelt right off), Iron Shell indicated he'd had a change of heart. With the trading completed, he and his men were ready to consider a drink of whiskey.

Tyler knew he'd be an old, old man before he forgot what happened next.

Captain Little cheerfully clapped Iron Shell on the shoulder, a gesture that caused a look of alarm to blaze in the chief's narrow black eyes. The captain smilingly directed the chief to the jug that rested on the beach. Iron Shell waved one of his men forward to fetch it, but when the Indian bent to pick it up, Bodie growled and snatched it away.

The brave seized the jug from Bodie's hands, and a second later a shot rang in the air. The brave fell to his knees, a look of surprise on his face, a round red hole in his forehead. He toppled forward without a sound. His fingers curled in the sand as if he were trying to hang on to something. He didn't move again.

Before a word could be said, an arrow struck Bodie

in the neck, severing an artery. He fell next to the man he'd just killed. The only other sound Tyler heard was the gentle sighing of the wind in the bare branches of the cottonwoods beside the river. Bodie's blood pumped out of the hole in his neck and vanished in the sand. In the meat-stained fingers of his right hand he still clutched the butt of a small pistol he'd pulled out of his pocket less than a minute before.

"Oh, sweet Jesus!" Isaac groaned. "This goin' to cause more trouble'n old Job ever dreamed about!"

Iron Shell scooped up his pelts. The other Indians marched to the skiff and gathered up all the goods they'd previously rejected—every pot and pan they could lay hands on, each bolt of cloth, every box of beads. Then Iron Shell, his black eyes hot, drew a long, thin-bladed knife from his belt. He advanced toward Captain Little.

Tyler was amazed to see that the cheery glow never left Captain Little's blue eyes. He was as agreeable and smiley as ever, as if any minute he might begin to hum "Turkey in the Straw" or make a joke. He held his hand up, palm out, just as Iron Shell had done when he refused a drink of whiskey.

"Hold on a minute, Chief," Tyler heard the captain say. His small eyes in their nests of puckered flesh were crafty but still twinkly. The smile that turned up the corners of his plump red lips caused the ends of his white mustache to twitch, like a cat's whiskers.

He spoke to the chief partly in Iron Shell's language, partly with sign language, partly in English. "This lad here," Tyler heard Captain Little say, directing the chief's attention to himself, "take him in place of your dead warrior."

Tyler couldn't believe what he'd just heard. Iron Shell turned a fierce-eyed glare in his direction, chilling Tyler to the bone. The chief's lip curled. He plainly considered that exchanging a fine, strong Sioux brave for a skinny, freckled white boy was an idiot's bargain.

"Take the other one, too," the captain offered generously. His voice was silky and affable. "My friend, I promise you these two boys will be far more valuable to you than this old man's poor, worthless carcass. You can easily swap the pair of 'em to another tribe for at least a dozen fine, fast ponies." He calmly lit his pipe and went on to explain a second advantage of the offer.

"Better yet, you can ransom that white one to the gov'mint people at one of the forts. As you know, white folks don't cotton to seein' one of their own taken captive by Indians. I reckon they'll pay handsomely to get him back."

Tyler flinched as Iron Shell gave him a more calculating appraisal. Then the chief studied Isaac with a puzzled frown. For the first time in his life, Tyler wished he'd been born black, that he was less desirable as a hostage. He quickly saw that wasn't exactly how Iron Shell viewed the matter.

First, the chief grabbed Tyler's arm and squeezed, as if inspecting it for muscle. With the tip of his knife, he lifted Tyler's hat, noted his hair, and seemed satisfied it was a suitably light color.

But when he turned to Isaac, the chief's eyes brightened. He examined Isaac's hair, stroking Isaac's tight black curls several times as if pleased by their texture. Next, he examined Isaac's skin, murmuring with delight. With the heel of his hand, he rubbed vigorously to remove the color from Isaac's arm. He quit only after Isaac squawked with pain.

A short conversation with Captain Little ensued. Tyler realized he and Isaac were about to be handed over to atone for the Indian brave's sudden death. Only the good Lord knew the kind of fate that awaited them. Isaac's reading of his bowels had been right. Captain Little had a heart even blacker than Satan's.

"You can't do this!" Tyler yelled, recovering from a paralysis of disbelief.

"We kept our end of the bargain!" he rattled on. Panic raised his voice several notches. "We cooked and fetched wood! We poled and rowed! I got you fresh meat every time you wanted it! You said you'd keep my money safe so nobody could steal it! Isaac and me never asked for favors, never complained! You can't turn the tables on us now—"

"Why, of course I can, laddie," the captain interrupted smoothly. It was plain he considered the transaction to be rather ordinary. Tyler stared at the old man, unable to believe what he saw. Even now, a traitor to the core, Captain Little still looked as kindly as St. Nicholas himself.

"You can see the nasty predicament I'm in, laddie," the captain explained, a hint of apology in his voice. "I'm in business to do business, which don't include payin' with my life for what that fool Bodie done." He laid his hand on Tyler's shoulder and massaged it affectionately, as if they were parting under the most agreeable circumstances.

"I'm getting long in the tooth, sonny, and made foolish mistakes in my youth," he admitted. "If I aim to provide for my old age, I got to do it now, seein' I only got a couple more years left to ply the Missouri with my old tub. So be a good lad—go along with Iron Shell—and don't raise a fuss about it."

He smiled into Tyler's eyes, his blue ones as friendly as ever. "Consider this a grand adventure you'll be able to regale your family with when your hair's as white as mine!"

A grand adventure? If Tyler hadn't been so scared that he'd almost wet his pants, he might have laughed.

Before he could do anything, however, Iron Shell grabbed him and shoved him up the beach. The chief's second in command, an Indian with a profile as sharp as a hatchet, did the same with Isaac. Their wrists and ankles were bound with leather thongs, then they were thrown like sacks of flour, heads down, across the backs of two ponies. The dead brave was lifted off the sand

and placed across the pony he'd ridden earlier.

Just before the horses were whipped into a gallop, Tyler heard Sooner howl desperately from the deck of the *Darlin' Nell.* The horse under him broke into a hard run (Tyler caught a flash of brown hide covered with white spots), and Sooner's cries were quickly drowned out by the drum of hoofbeats. Except for Isaac, Tyler realized he was parting company with everything he'd come west with—Sooner . . . Elway's rifle . . . his money.

Betrayed. Such a short, hard word couldn't do justice to the crime Captain Little had just committed.

Chapter Eight

Tyler's ribs cracked as the spotted pony's sharp spine cut into his middle, sawing him nearly in half.

In no time, his cap fell off and cartwheeled away in the dust. Hanging upside down made the blood rush to his head, causing a terrible throb behind his eyes. After half a mile, the roast venison he'd been chomping on when the Sioux appeared on the bluff boiled up from his belly and splattered down the pony's flanks.

Tyler was too miserable to wonder how Isaac was faring. After a few more miles—head pounding, ribs that seemed to puncture his lungs, vomit-stench thick in his nostrils, he willingly let himself drift into half-consciousness.

As blue evening shadows fell across the prairie, Tyler was roused from his stupor as he was rudely jerked off the pony's back. He was dumped unceremoniously on the ground not far from a large fire.

His mouth, eyes, and nose were clogged with dust from the journey. The dried vomit in his hair was stiff and crusty. Blood had pooled thicker than beeswax at the top of his head. His arms and legs were as useless as dead tree limbs. Was he alive? Dead? Soon to be killed? Tyler didn't care.

Rough hands hoisted him to his feet and cut the thongs from his ankles but not the ones around his wrists. Tyler was dimly aware that nearby Isaac was jerked upright as well.

All around, the chatter of voices in a strange tongue indicated great excitement at the sight of the captives. Yet moments later the air was filled with the sound of women's shrill voices raised in a lament. Tyler knew without being told that it must be a death chant for the man Bodie had killed.

Tyler pawed clumsily at his dirt-filled eyes. He blinked fast to clear his vision. "Isaac, you all right?" he croaked.

"Alive, that's all I know," Isaac answered.

Iron Shell prodded the boys through the half-dark toward the center of what Tyler saw was a large circle of tipis. Small children, their black eyes bright with curiousity, crowded close to pick at his clothes or pinch his arms and legs. It was clear, though, that it was Isaac who was of greatest interest.

As the red haze slowly cleared from his eyes, Tyler heard a single voice replace the chatter of many. It was Iron Shell's, explaining to his people what had happened back at the cove.

Although he couldn't understand the words, Tyler saw the tale unfold as the chief reenacted the murder in lively pantomime—how Bodie snatched the jug of whiskey away even though the captain had offered it . . . how Bodie pulled the pistol from his pocket . . . a shot rang out . . . a wound bloomed on the warrior's forehead. How seconds later an arrow was sent through Bodie's neck, and these two captives were traded for the dead man. Through it all, from beyond the circle of orange light cast by the fire, the women's grieving wails punctuated Iron Shell's story.

"These folks is plenty peeved about what happened," Isaac whispered. "Shows what whiskey can do—made a fool of Bodie and prisoners outta you and me."

When Tyler turned to look at his friend, it was to see Isaac was coated with white from top to toe. Pale dust layered on his black skin created an apparition from hell: Isaac's cheeks were ghostly; he had a pair of black holes for eyes. A slash marked his mouth; his hair was so filled with dust, it was the color of ash. But before Isaac could brush himself off, Iron Shell seized him and led him closer to the fire.

With the tender care that a person would use to brush dirt off a sacred object, the chief solemnly cleaned

Isaac's arms, hands, and face with the tail of his own plaid shirt. Again he stroked Isaac's head, plucking at the tight black curls with delight. He exclaimed with amazement at the color of Isaac's skin, and invited everyone else to inspect it, even to rub off the color if they could.

Isaac endured the examination for several minutes, but when he yelped and hugged his arms to his body, Iron Shell waved the onlookers aside. He carefully checked the flesh of his new treasure to be sure it wasn't damaged, then patted Isaac's shoulder.

Only then did Iron Shell drag Tyler forward. His voice took on an entirely different tone. It sounded as businesslike as Captain Little's had a few hours earlier. Tyler deduced from the chief's gestures that he was explaining that—being a white boy—he could be traded for money at one of the forts. Tyler felt a stab of disappointment. It was plain he wasn't considered a treasure, like Isaac.

Which was bad enough, but when Tyler noted how frequently the chief's glance (in a short time it seemed to have become almost fond) strayed in Isaac's direction, it dawned on him that Iron Shell had no intention of giving up a boy whose skin was the amazing color of charred log.

So far, he'd been parted from Elway's rifle, his money, and a loyal dog, and now it was plain to Tyler that he and Isaac would eventually be parted, too. *He* would be ransomed back to the whites; Isaac would be kept because he was special.

The aroma rising from a pot over the fire reminded Tyler he wasn't having a nightmare. It smelled foreign, but having lost everything he'd eaten hours ago, he felt a twinge of hunger. Someone—a woman whose face was hidden by shadows—pressed a large tin cup in his hands, while someone else did the same for Isaac.

Iron Shell gestured to them to eat, encouraging them by crying, *"Ayasota, ayasota!* Eat up, eat up!" No spoons or forks were offered, so when Isaac lifted the cup to his lips, Tyler did likewise. In the firelight, he could see the stuff was dark brown, the color of sorghum. He gagged, filled with revulsion at the thought of what it might be. Boiled dog? His appetite vanished.

Isaac wasn't squeamish. He slurped up his meal and when he licked the rim of the cup, cries of approval erupted from everyone gathered around. Tyler tried to do the same, but nearly strangled. As far as he could tell, the concoction was mostly small pieces of greasy meat (dogs weren't so greasy, were they?) and some kind of vegetable that tasted almost like an onion.

Inside Iron Shell's tipi, which was warmed by a small fire glowing in the center, Tyler and Isaac were made to understand they must lie on the ground for the night. Their hands were left securely bound.

It also was clear they must take places on opposite sides of the fire. Luckily, the floor of the dwelling was covered with various kinds of animal skins, but no blankets were offered. Two small boys—Tyler decided they must be Iron Shell's sons (they'd been among the children who gave him hard pinches earlier)—crawled into their parents' bed, which was piled high with more skins and furs.

Then Iron Shell spoke to his wife. In a moment, Isaac was given a buffalo robe tanned smooth on the inside and covered with thick dark hair on the outside. The woman laid it hair-side down over him.

Tyler waited. Nothing was offered to him. He groaned softly and chewed on his knuckles. Even with a covering of skins, the earth beneath his back was as bumpy as a cobbled road. Just the same, after the horrendous trip when he'd been draped like a sack of meal over the back of a sharp-spined horse, it felt almost comfortable.

Tyler waited till he was sure Iron Shell and his wife were asleep, then lifted himself on one elbow. "Isaac?" he called softly across the glowing embers of the fire.

"I'm here, Ty. I'd share this here cover wit' you but—"

Before Isaac could say another word, Tyler felt himself rapped smartly on the head with a stick. A woman's voice exclaimed something that sounded like, *"Hiya, hiya!"* He didn't need to be told it meant, "No, no!"

He eased himself back onto the lumpy ground and waited for sleep to overtake him. In the morning he'd find a way to talk to Isaac. It would be important to figure out what they should do next, before Iron Shell had a chance to split them up.

Tyler watched the firelight flicker on the walls of Iron

Shell's tipi. His heart ached, not for his lost possessions, not even for the money. Only for Sooner. Till he died, Tyler knew he'd never forget the dog's desperate cry from the bow of the *Darlin' Nell*. So far, the only good thing to be said about the situation he and Isaac were in was they weren't dead. Yet.

"Some men aren't meant for safe pastures," Elway told Mama a few weeks ago. "Maybe Tyler is one of 'em, just like his papa before him." The words filled Tyler with a flash of panic. He dug feverishly in the pocket of his shirt.

Thank God! Papa's letter was still there, right over his heart. If he'd lost it—well, that would've been the last straw. He turned on his side so the fire could warm his back and buttocks. At last, sleep covered him with welcome dark wings.

Tyler woke with bones that had aged a hundred years overnight. Even after the first day of poling up the Missouri he hadn't ached so bad. The joints of his hips and shoulders felt frozen, the way a wheel that hasn't been greased in a long while gets frozen to a wagon hub. The pain in his ribs made it hard to take a deep breath. When he touched his breastbone it was so tender, he hastily lifted his fingers.

He raised his head. The fire that had glowed softly in the darkness last night was a bed of cold ash. The spot where Isaac's voice had come from was deserted. Iron

Shell himself still slept soundly beneath his pile of furs, but his wife and sons were gone.

Tyler let his gaze travel around the circular confines of the Sioux lodge. It was about twenty feet in diameter, though somewhat wider at the end farthest from the entrance, giving it an egg shape. Three poles, stripped clean of bark and polished smooth, were lashed together overhead and were the main support of the sewn-together buffalo hides that were stretched around the outside. Smaller poles, placed between the large ones, also met at the top, where an opening—off-center of being smack in the middle—showed a patch of autumn sky.

Boxes and bags and pouches made of leather, each decorated with beadwork, paintings, or dyed porcupine quills, were placed tidily around the perimeter of the lodge. What looked like a rawhide backrest sat not far from where Iron Shell slept. It certainly wasn't a regular house, not the kind with walls and shelves for dishes and an iron stove such as Mama would insist on, yet there was something almost cozy about it.

Outside, Tyler heard a murmur of voices. Two of them seemed to be the voices of small children. He got to his hands and knees and crawled noiselessly to where he saw light coming in around the edge of an oval-shaped tipi flap. When he drew it aside and peeked out, he saw the entrance faced east. The October day was clear and mild, and the rising sun had painted the other pale tipis in the Sioux village a warm, rosy color.

The woman whose face he hadn't seen last night was tending a cook fire in front of the tipi. She gave him a sharp look when she heard the whisper of leather-against-leather when the lodge flap was raised.

The woman's face was round, her eyes shrewd and no-nonsense, and her plump cheeks were as smooth and shiny as polished apples. The two small boys who squatted beside her, their knees tucked under their chins, stared at him. Tyler looked at one, then the other. Twins; only their parents could've told one from the other.

Isaac, crouched across the fire from the woman and her sons, gave Tyler a feeble smile. "We made it through the night, Ty," he whispered. "Hangin' head-down over them ponies yesterday I wondered if we'd ever see another sun come up." At the sound of Isaac's voice, the woman raised a wooden spoon from the pot she was stirring. She waggled it first at him, then at Tyler.

"Hiya!" she exclaimed, to warn them again about talking to each other. Tyler filed the word away in his mind. He might need it sometime. He glanced around at the Indian camp, and hoped the woman wouldn't rap him on the head for looking as well as talking.

Never in his wildest dreams had he ever imagined he'd end up as an Indian prisoner. And if your bowels had been as smart as Isaac's, he reminded himself, you wouldn't be! Because the captain had reminded him of St. Nicholas, he'd let himself believe the old man had the same good heart as a character in a Christmas story.

In front of every tipi, which Tyler noticed had been arranged like the chief's so that their entrances faced east, other women were as busy as Iron Shell's wife. Some of the women were old, some were about Mama's age, some were girls not much bigger than Rosa Lee. Each seemed to have a job to do—getting water from the nearby creek, bringing wood from a thicket of leafless trees behind the camp, or stirring stuff in a pot from which peculiar aromas wafted on the crisp morning air.

A trio of girls about his age passed by on their way to tipis on the far side of the camp circle, their arms full of sticks and dead branches. They giggled and ducked their heads behind their loads as they sneaked curious glances at him and Isaac. The tallest girl, whose braids were as thick as Tyler's wrist, pointed to her companions, indicating that Isaac was special. In spite of himself, Tyler felt another stab of envy.

"You and me been captives less'n twelve hours, Isaac, and already these folks got the idea you're some kind of prize pig!" Tyler muttered softly enough that Iron Shell's wife wouldn't hear. Isaac only smiled, but Tyler observed that it was a rather satisfied smile.

A rustling noise at the doorway of the lodge announced that Iron Shell had roused himself. In the confusion of yesterday, Tyler remembered a man who'd been the personification of ugly savagery. In the plain light of morning, however, he saw someone folks might

call handsome. The fact that Iron Shell *was* handsome—
In the same way Black Jack Bohannon had been—
surprised Tyler more than a little.

Of course Iron Shell wasn't as tall as Papa, but his
shoulders were broad and he carried his head high,
the same proud way Papa had. When he looked at a
person—and at that very moment he returned Tyler's
stare with a hard one of his own—the Sioux chief's
narrow black eyes bored two holes right through to the
other side. The moment he sat cross-legged by the fire,
however, his sons crawled over him like a pair of bear
cubs, and the chief's face softened with affection.

Iron Shell and his wife commenced to talk, gesturing
now and then at the captives. The woman filled a bowl
with whatever she'd been stirring in the pot and carried
it to Isaac.

Tyler saw goodwill in her glance as she presented it
to him. She reached out to pat Isaac's hair, laughing out-
right when she felt its texture. She peered at the long
scar on his face and touched it curiously with the tip of
her finger. Then she filled a second bowl and plunked it
down in front of Tyler with scarcely a glance at any part
of him.

How peculiar, Tyler thought. In the space of a few
short hours he and Isaac had switched places! He gritted his teeth and tried to understand how such a thing
could have happened. Well, the Indians had colored
skins themselves, didn't they, so maybe the turnabout in

his and Isaac's fortunes made sense. Being white, *he* was the one who now was a second-class citizen.

Tyler peered into the bowl he'd been given. Whatever it was, it looked disgusting. He dared a glance in Isaac's direction, to see how he was handling breakfast. Isaac returned his gaze with a familiar lopsided smile, and Tyler smiled back. It wasn't Isaac's fault that their fortunes had been switched. It was as unexpected as getting kidnapped; there was no cause to blame Isaac for it.

Isaac ate his meal by picking up chunks of it between thumb and forefinger and inspecting them none too closely. Tyler imitated him. Actually, the stuff didn't taste too bad. Again, it was greasier than the kind of food Mama cooked, but if he planned to make a run for it, Tyler realized he'd have to keep up his strength. Starting now, he'd eat whatever was put in front of him and wouldn't think twice about what it was, no matter how it tasted.

The two little boys, their dark eyes and round faces so identical, they were mirror images of each other, giggled behind their hands and imitated the fussy way Tyler ate. Then, shyly, they crept closer to Isaac and did what their mother had done. They touched his skin, reached up to stroke his hair, and inspected the scar on his cheek.

Tyler ate till his bowl was clean. No way would he let himself be jealous of the attention that was paid to Isaac. He was so different, the Indians couldn't help but be fascinated. Besides, in a little while it wouldn't matter one way or the other who was favored and who wasn't. Only a day ago they were trying to escape from Captain Little. Now they had to escape from the Sioux.

CHAPTER NINE

What happened to people after they got captured by Indians?

The first night Tyler spent in Iron Shell's tipi he was too scared and tired to care. Breakfast was scarcely over the next morning, before he discovered the answer was simple. It probably didn't surprise Isaac at all.

They became slaves.

Slaves didn't tend pony herds, because that would give them a chance to escape. Slaves weren't sent out with hunting parties, either, which required a weapon that might be turned against their captors. Instead, slaves were put to doing the work of women—exactly what no proud, self-respecting Sioux man or boy would ever consider doing.

Tyler and Isaac had no sooner finished eating whatever was in their breakfast bowls than several older boys from the village gathered in front of Iron Shell's lodge. They arrived in pairs or groups of three and four, as if by a prearranged agreement with their chief.

Tyler eyed them warily. They were about his and Isaac's age, but most looked more like half-grown men than any boys he'd known back home. Although there was a sharp chill in the air, these boys wore only breechclouts and mocassins. Their arms and legs were roped with muscle, and they moved lightly on the balls of their feet. They treated each other with the easy familiarity of those who'd shared hard times as well as good ones.

After a discussion with Iron Shell, the lean, flint-eyed boy who seemed to be the leader of the group gestured to Tyler and Isaac to get to their feet. They were herded along, shoved or pushed from time to time in a way that wasn't exactly mean but it wasn't friendly, either.

In the patch of woods from which the wood-toting girls had come earlier, he and Isaac were put to work collecting broken branches and chunks of windfall that could be hauled back to camp. The Indian boys supervised them as if they were livestock, nudging each other and laughing among themselves.

Tyler set his jaw. It was unnerving not to know what they found so comical. He glanced at Isaac to get a sense of how he was taking such treatment. Isaac's dark face was stony. If his blood was boiling, there was no way to tell. He's had a lot more practice being a slave than I have, Tyler decided. Me, I don't cotton to this. No sir, not a doggone bit!

In a short time the trio of girls returned, each carrying what looked to be a leather pouch that she filled with water from the nearby creek. The Indian boys waved their arms and called out greetings, making the girls giggle and duck their heads to hide their delight.

Tyler remembered the horseplay that went on among the older kids at the school yard back home. It surprised him a little that Sioux boys and girls flirted, too. Oat Snepp had big eyes for Sallyjo McCarthy, and to impress her one day he put on a big show of jumping over the fence that separated the school yard from Cooper's cow pasture. He got his pants caught, ripped them up the backside so that everybody could see his underwear. He was sent home for the rest of the day, holding his britches together as he ran down the road.

Tyler's gaze was drawn again to the tallest girl of the threesome. She was about the same height he was himself. Did it mean she was about fourteen, too? Were the two shorter girls her younger sisters? He couldn't help but admire her thick dark hair and the easy way she moved inside her buckskin dress.

Quickly he shrugged off an interest in her. It didn't matter one way or the other whether he admired her or not. She didn't speak English, and he couldn't speak Sioux. Anyway, with luck he and Isaac would be gone before there'd be time to have any other thoughts about her.

The following day began the same way. The Indian boys, led by the sharp-eyed one who was their leader, showed up at Iron Shell's tipi in the morning, collected their prisoners, then Tyler and Isaac were herded toward the woods like a pair of oxen.

Tyler didn't mind working, though. It helped pass the time, but soon it began to annoy him that he was the one—far oftener than Isaac—who was singled out for most of the shoving and pushing. When the Sioux boys laughed loudest, Tyler realized he was the one in particular they were laughing at. They were like Iron Shell's wife: They made no secret about favoring Isaac.

I ain't goin' to let it bother me, though, Tyler told himself silently. In a few days, me and Isaac'll be miles away from here. All we need is a chance to be alone together long enough to get some kind of plan figured out. Then this slave business will be over for both of us and things between him and me will be just like they were before.

Four days later, though, before escape plans could be made, Isaac became more admired than ever. He whupped He Wonjetah, or One Horn, the leader of the Indian boys, in a wrestling match.

The contest between them began more or less innocently, as scraps on school yards usually did. To impress the three girls when they showed up with their buffalo-stomach water pouches every morning, One Horn had taken to pushing both of his prisoners into the creek. The sight of Tyler and Isaac tumbling head over heels into the water caused great glee among the boys and roused snickers of admiring laughter from the girls.

When the girls approached on the fourth morning, Tyler knew another dousing was coming. He knew it couldn't be avoided, so with a groan he let himself be shoved end-over-teakettle into the sparkling, October-cold water. He crawled up the creek bank soaking wet, his arms covered with purple goose bumps. If he was lucky, his clothes might be dry by nightfall. If not, he'd go to sleep half-damp and shivering.

For some reason, though, Isaac suddenly had a change of heart. He flat out refused to be dunked again.

Instead, he squared off at One Horn, his legs braced wide. The expression on Isaac's face was one Tyler had never seen before. It was as if he remembered that he was a freed boy now, that he didn't need to be beholden to anybody, not even a Sioux bully named One Horn. Isaac clenched his teeth so hard, the muscle at the corner of each jaw popped out like a walnut under his dark skin. Resentment turned the scar on his cheek into a blazing red slash.

When One Horn—a shade taller than Isaac, with longer arms—reached out to give Isaac a second harder shove, Isaac surprised him by unexpectedly leaping forward and seizing his tormenter in a bear hug. One Horn struggled to get away, but Isaac only held on fast, squeezing him around the middle so hard, the Indian boy opened his mouth, his tongue hanging out, and gasped for breath.

Tyler's heart hammered as he waited for One Horn's cronies to come to their leader's rescue. They didn't move a hair. Instead, the Sioux boys stood with arms crossed and watched silently, their black eyes bright with amusement as the struggle went on. It was plain they wanted to see who would be victorious, but that it was up to One Horn himself to get the best of Isaac if he could.

Tyler noticed that Isaac was careful not to hurt One Horn too bad. Gasping and choking, One Horn thrashed this way and that. The cords on his neck stood out as he tried to strike Isaac with his fists. Finally, he ceased to struggle and let himself go limp inside Isaac's bear hug. Only then did Isaac turn him loose and set him upright.

Lordy, lordy! One Horn's gonna pick up the rock that's right next to his right foot and knock Isaac's brains out, Tyler thought. Fear made his mouth dry. He forgot that he'd been a little peeved lately about Isaac being favored by everyone, because if anything happened to him . . .

Instead of picking up the rock or the tree branch that lay a little farther away, One Horn acknowledged Isaac's victory with a rueful shrug. "Okiya," he said, "okiya."

He tapped Isaac's shoulder and made a sign meaning they ought to be friends.

Tyler stared, amazed. The other boys gathered around Isaac, expressing their approval with sign language and laughter. There was no doubt that Isaac, as black as could be, now enjoyed the privileges that Tyler had once taken for granted—of being first, of being most important. Here, in Iron Shell's camp, the certainties of his old white world had been turned upside down.

After the fight with One Horn, Isaac got off easier than ever, while Tyler found himself working every day till his muscles cried out for the horse linament Papa rubbed on Red Ransom after a long day's ride. Each night, he collapsed on the hard ground inside Iron Shell's tipi, too tired to dwell very long on how the tables had been turned.

Yet he couldn't resist complaining to Isaac on the rare morning when they had a moment to themselves. "I don't know why One Horn's got it in for me and not you," he groused.

"It's on account of it was his uncle that Bodie shot," Isaac explained. "He was killed by a white man—and you be white, too. In One Horn's mind he holds you responsible, even though you didn't do it yourself. He aims to settle the debt, one way or the other."

"What about Iron Shell's wife? She's got it in for me, too."

Isaac grinned. "Ooaya told me she had no daughters to help her," he said. "Her sons must grow up to be brave warriors, so she's decided you're goin' to be the daughter she never had."

"Ooaya? How'd you find out her name?"

"She told me." Now Isaac and Iron Shell's wife were gabbing together like a pair of old chums!

"Well, I ain't a girl," Tyler snapped. Bitterness tasted sour in his mouth. "And I sure don't appreciate being treated like one!"

Back in Missouri, hadn't he stuck up for Isaac lots of times—in front of Mama, Mr. Blackburn, Oat Snepp, the manager of the Oaklee Inn, not to mention the hemp buyer? Sure, he had—so when was Isaac going to return the favor?

Tyler's resentment doubled when he discovered Ooaya wasn't the only one who was teaching Isaac Indian words. One Horn and his cronies were giving him lessons in Sioux as well. It was Isaac himself who proudly reported it.

"Look up there, Ty," he said, pointing skyward as they headed for the woods one morning. "We call that the sun. These folks call it *wi*."

"*Wi*, pee, flea!" Tyler retorted through clenched teeth. "Ain't it enough I'm the one who gets stuck doing all the work? Quit acting like a know-it-all."

"Aw, don't get a sore head, Ty," Isaac chided gently. "It was you who taught me how to write my name, remember? You taught me how words looked on paper—easy little words like *dog* and *mule* and *barn*. Now I aim to do the same for you—to pass on to you everything I learn. Deep down, you know Isaac ain't actin' smart for the sake of actin' smart."

Tyler sighed. It had never been his nature to have a spiteful disposition, and he didn't like having one now. It made him act mean, like Cousin Clayton. He hated to think he might end up as big a pain in the neck as Clayton.

"All right, so what else they been teaching you?" Tyler asked, making his voice light. After all, knowing some Indian words might come in handy. It made sense to take advantage of everything Isaac had learned.

"My skin—you an' me call it black—but the Sioux call it *sapa*. I told 'em there's no way they can rub that color offa me, so they finally quit trying," Isaac admitted with a chuckle.

"An' you—you be a white boy, a *wasichu*." Isaac pulled up his shirt to show his belly button. "*C'ekpa*," he announced, pointing. Next, he tapped his head with the flat of his hand. "This is my *p'a nata*," he said, so tickled by the chance to show off that his grin got wider than a shoebox.

"Some education!" Tyler snorted. "So you know the name of the sun, a black skin, a belly button, and a head—what kind of sentence can a person string together outta that?"

Isaac wasn't finished reciting everything he knew. "Know what else One Horn told me?"

Tyler refused to ask.

"That I'm *mawaste*," Isaac announced. He puffed out his chest.

"What's that mean?"

"Means 'I am good.' That's what One Horn told me after we had our tussle there by the creek—*mawaste*, that I was good. Anyway, I'll learn as much as those boys be willin' to teach me, Ty, and I'll pass it all on to you. So don't you go feelin' hard-hearted and bitter agin ol' Isaac. He ain't gonna betray you, no way."

Tyler sighed and looped his arm around Isaac's shoulder. Isaac was right, of course. He wasn't acting smart for the sake of acting smart. He's the only friend I got in this wild country, Tyler realized. If I harden my heart against him, I'll be making a big mistake.

The only crime that had been committed against him—against Isaac, too, for that matter—was the act of one man: Captain Richard Little. Tyler clamped his lips tight. No matter how long it took, he'd get even with that old buzzard someday.

Tyler had counted ten sunrises at Iron Shell's village when he woke one morning to discover an even deeper chill in the air than other mornings. No longer was it simply cool. The air was downright frigid, cold enough to make a person want to stay indoors all day.

As if the change in the weather had been awaited by everyone in camp, when Tyler and Isaac crawled out of the tipi they saw that a move was underway. Many tipis had already been struck, or collapsed, wrapped around their tipi poles, then tied with other household possessions, food, and clothing onto travois poles pulled by ponies. The dogs in the camp ran about, barking and stealing food when they could, while small children like Iron Shell's sons became giddy with excitement.

The women seemed to be in charge of the business of moving, while the men and boys rounded up the horse herd. Tyler was relieved when One Horn and his buddies mounted up to go with the men, leaving him and Isaac under the watchful eye of Ooaya. She might rap him on the head for talking, Tyler thought, but at least she wouldn't throw him in a creek. Now, for the first time, he and Isaac might have a chance to talk about an escape plan.

When Ooaya was ready to follow the others, she lifted her twin sons on top of the load. She mounted the pony to which the travois poles were attached, and motioned to Tyler and Isaac to follow close beside her so she could keep a watchful eye on them.

What would she have done if he and Isaac had run off into the woods? Tyler wondered. But what good would that do? He and Isaac had no food or any warm clothes, yet cold weather was on the way. They didn't even know where they were, or how far they were from the Missouri River.

For now, their best hope was to remain captives until they'd worked out a way to survive once they were on their own. A gust of cold air swept up the thin sleeves of Tyler's shirt, reminding him that snow would soon be coming. Besides, any plan they came up with had to include horses. One for him, one for Isaac, so they could cover greater distances faster.

Tyler dropped back a pace and waited to see if Ooaya noticed. When she didn't, he signaled Isaac to do the same. He inclined his head to the left, where a dust cloud raised by the pony herd hid the herders from view.

"We got to figure out a way to get a couple of those for you and me," he whispered.

"Horses? Easier said than done," Isaac murmured. "One Horn says them ponies are guarded day and night. The enemies of the Sioux—he called 'em *hohes,* warriors from the Crow tribe—make raids on the horse herds every chance they get." Isaac lifted an eyebrow.

"Anyway, what'd happen if we got caught stealin' horses? I reckon these folks don't take any kindlier to horse thieves than white men do. Iron Shell ain't killed us yet—but he might if we try to steal his ponies."

Tyler pushed such a fate out of his mind. What bothered him more was that Isaac didn't seem interested in making plans to get away as quick as possible.

"It ain't started to snow yet, Isaac, but it's important to get away from here before it does," Tyler pointed out. "Once snow's on the ground, we'll be easier to track than a couple dumb rabbits. It'd take Iron Shell less'n ten minutes to catch us. But if we could get away now—"

Tyler lifted his nose into the wind. An almost-sweet scent filled his nostrils. Some folks didn't believe a person could smell snow on the air, but Papa had told him otherwise. "It's a clean smell," he'd said. "Crisp around the edges, sort of like the first apple you bite into in the fall."

"We probably have only a couple days to make our move," Tyler insisted. "We got to do some quick thinking, Isaac."

Ooaya noticed they'd fallen behind, and with peevish gestures ordered them to move up beside her. Tyler grimaced. Devising a plan would have to be postponed. Besides, it was plain that Isaac needed more convincing.

Before night fell, a new camp was made. Like the one before it, this one had a creek nearby. A thicket of woods to the northwest cut the bite of the prevailing wind and provided wood for fuel. Alas, in the morning, Tyler discovered that his nose had been right.

The woods were covered with three inches of soft, heavy snow, so white that he had to squint against its glare. The cottonwoods wore ghostly shrouds; the pines were so weighted down, their branches dipped low to the ground, creating dark caves next to their trunks. Snow fell all day, hissing in the coals of the fire that Ooaya tended.

Tyler's heart sank. It was going to be a long winter.

CHAPTER TEN

After the snow fell, One Horn and his friends gave up their breechclouts for trousers made of leather. Their deerskin shirts, sometimes decorated with beads and embroidered with porcupine quills dyed yellow, blue, and red, were fringed at the lower edges. The boys' caps, trimmed with fur (Tyler thought it looked like rabbit hair), protected their heads from the cold.

Tyler remembered the sturdy brown jacket Mama gave him for his trip west, the three pairs of warm wool socks she'd knitted, and the winter cap she made with flaps that folded over his ears. She's given Isaac one of Papa's old coats and knitted socks for him, too. All had been left aboard the *Darlin' Nell*. No doubt they were keeping others warm at this very moment.

But on that first cold morning, Ooaya dug into one of the leather bundles Tyler had helped her load onto her travois poles during the move. She lifted out a shirt for Isaac. It wasn't new, no more than Papa's coat had been, and she set about patching it. Tyler watched her present it to Isaac with a flourish. She even added a cap, trimmed with fur like One Horn's.

After casting crabby glances in his direction and grumbling in her put-upon way, Ooaya dug out a second garment. It was even more worn than the one she'd given Isaac. She inspected it, turning it this way and that, decided not to mend it, and tossed it to Tyler.

He caught it in midair. Before Mama married Elway, he mused, he'd been the oldest boy, which gave him special privileges. He came first, so his clothes were always new. His current predicament made him wonder (he had to admit he'd never given it a moment's thought before) how Lucas felt about getting hand-me-downs all his life. Tyler wished he'd asked Mama to give Lucas something new every now and then, something never worn by anyone else and meant for him alone.

Now, Tyler was far too cold to be picky. He shrugged himself into the old shirt, noting that even with a rip partway down one side it was surprisingly warm. The worn buckskin was as soft as the piece of blue velvet Mama once used to make a bonnet for Rosa Lee. Of course, for him there wasn't any warm hat trimmed with fur. Instead, Ooaya held up a raggedy green-and-brown wool scarf that probably had belonged to a white person once upon a time.

Tyler accepted it without complaint. *"Philamayaye,"* he said, *"philamayaye,"* and was glad Isaac had taught him how to say "thank you." Tyler tied the scarf over his head and tucked the ends inside the collar of the leather shirt. He wondered uneasily what had happened to its the owner. He pushed the question—and its answer—out of his mind.

The important thing was it would keep his ears from freezing, withering, then turning black like the ears of the old yellow tomcat that showed up at Sweet Creek in the dead of winter one year. The tips of its ears finally fell off, leaving only nubbins. Ever after, Papa called it Stubs.

The women of Iron Shell's village had stored plenty of dried meat in their *parfleches,* or rawhide food cases, but on the fifth day in the new camp, hunters were able to bring down three deer that had been easy to track through the fresh snow.

The prospect of fresh-killed meat caused a mood of jubilation to spread through the camp. The dogs began to fight among themselves as soon as the men dragged the animals into camp. Tyler and Isaac watched the women butcher the carcasses, singing a trilling song of thanksgiving as the entrails steamed in the cold air. When their job was done, the meat was divided equally among all the families in the village.

"Ain't nobody ever left to go hungry around here," Isaac said admiringly. None of the animal parts were wasted, either, as Tyler learned firsthand when Ooaya set him to work. The stomachs of the creatures were emptied and rinsed to become new water bags. The guts were washed, to be used as casings for a sausage concoction made of shredded meat, dried chokecherries, and tallow.

The hide of one of the deer was still wet when Ooaya handed Tyler a scraper and showed him how to use it. She set a pair of the horns aside and told him with sign language that she would make pieces of it into buttons and a necklace. The leg bones were cracked so marrow could be removed. Other parts of the animals—hearts, livers, lungs, and tongues—also were shared among the womenfolk.

Late in the day, everyone gathered around a large central fire to celebrate a community feast. A sense of well-being radiated through the village that was as warm as the blaze that everyone gathered around. Even though he was a prisoner, Tyler felt joy creep into his bones. He didn't steel his heart against it, but let himself be caught up, too. After all, there was much to be thankful for: He was warm; he and Isaac were still together; soon they'd be eating fresh venison.

Only one thing would have made the moment perfect. If only Sooner were here, Tyler thought. His sorrow felt like a knife that had been slipped between his ribs. His spirits sagged, as they always did whenever he thought of Bigger's son, until he realized he was standing only an arm's length from the tall girl with the long, thick braids.

She noticed him at the same moment, and turned to look at him with an expression Tyler couldn't fathom. He knew she wasn't being coy, though. Sallyjo McCarthy back home, who'd laughed louder than anyone at the sight of Oat Snepp's underwear, taught Tyler everything he knew about girls who flirted. There was nothing coquettish about the Indian girl's glance. Instead, it was so piercing that Tyler began to squirm.

She studied each of his features as if, separately or together, they were objects of unusual interest. She'd probably never seen a white person up close, he decided, and was curious. Yet when she peered directly into his eyes, Tyler had an eerie sense that she was trying to look deep inside him, as if she expected to find something she'd lost and had been searching for. But before he could make a friendly sign to her, her friends swept her away with merry cries, and she disappeared in the crowd.

When Tyler lay down that night, he discovered— wonder of wonders!—Ooaya had laid out a worn blanket for him. He folded it gratefully about himself. With his belly full of venison and sleep about to descend, he let his thoughts drift back to the way the Indian girl had looked at him. He almost smiled in the dark. He hoped Isaac had learned some new Sioux words. No way could he have a conversation with her using *wi, sapa,* and *c'ekpa*—sun, black, and belly button!

• • •

"C'mon, Ty!" Isaac called after breakfast the next morning. "We're goin' to go sledding!"

Tyler glanced up from his task of hide scraping. "You joshing me or what?" he muttered. Isaac didn't have to scrape hides; he was free to fool around all day, doing whatever pleased him. "You must be crazy. These folks don't have sleds."

"Why, sure they do," Isaac countered. "'Course, they don't call the contraption a sled. To them, it's a *hohukazunta.* Come and see!" Using elaborate sign language, Isaac begged Ooaya to let Tyler come along. In the air, he pantomimed sledding down a slope with such animation that she laughed out loud. Ooaya plucked the hide scraper out of Tyler's hands and waved him off with a good-natured shrug.

One Horn and his friends had gathered at the top of a long, smooth slope beyond the south edge of the woods. The sleds Isaac talked about were nothing like the wooden ones Tyler remembered he and Lucas had at Sweet Creek. These were made from the curved ribs of a buffalo. The ribs were lashed together with rawhide thongs in a shallow, dishlike shape, almost as if they'd been fashioned from barrel staves. Each sled had a leather steering rein at the front. A rider stood upright with one foot on the dish, then pushed off with the other.

Right away, Isaac was invited to compete in a race

down the hill. One Horn gave him instructions, speaking Sioux and demonstrating how to steer the sled. Another boy stood upright on the second sled, and an instant later Isaac went flying down the slope. He arrived at the bottom first, to the cheers of the spectators.

As Tyler waited for Isaac to trudge back up with the sled under his arm, he saw several girls gather at the bottom of the hill to watch the fun. He searched the crowd for the face of the one who'd looked deep into his eyes the night before. It was impossible to miss her, because she was so much taller than her companions. When she caught his glance, Tyler felt his face get warm. Sallyjo McCarthy's glances never made him blush. Why was he turning red now?

This girl's only an Indian, Tyler reminded himself. Besides, you're not going to be around much longer, so what does it matter if she looks at you as if she wants to know you better? Before he could turn away, the girl waved her companions to follow her and they all trekked to the top of the hill.

Once again, Tyler found himself standing within an arm's length of her. She turned to him and inspected his face carefully, feature by feature, freckle by freckle. He tried to smile, wondering what someone like Elway Snepp would do in a situation like this. Elway was so polite—he'd raise his hat, that's what he'd do. But Tyler was wearing Ooaya's ratty old scarf. To lift it would be plain silly, so he kept smiling and halfway hoped she'd find someone else to stare at.

Instead, the girl studied him more closely than before. Tyler felt his armpits get wet. She parted her lips as if she intended to speak, but no sound sound came out.

The truth dawned on Tyler like a clap of thunder: Why, she was mute and deaf! That's why she stared at him so hard, like poor Old Man Knauss back home, who read lips and watched your face so close, you wondered if there was a booger hanging out your nose.

When the girl spoke, Tyler was transfixed with shock.

"My . . . name . . . is . . ." she began. Each word was rusty, as if she hadn't used it in a long, long time.

Tyler's jaw dropped. He snapped it shut, too stunned to make a sound himself.

"My . . . name . . . is . . ." the girl began again. She concentrated hard, drawing her brows together, shaping each word carefully. "My . . . name is . . . Mary . . . Burden."

"Greatgodamighty!" Tyler exclaimed softly. "You speak English!"

The girl nodded. "I am called . . . Many Horses now. But a long time ago . . . I was named . . . Mary Burden."

"How long you been here?" Tyler asked, dropping his voice to a softer whisper.

"Many summers," answered Mary Burden. Her

words were still rusty, but began to come more easily. "Many winters, too. It seems as if . . ." She hesitated again. "It seems as if . . . I've lived here . . . forever."

"These folks kidnap you, or what?"

"I wasn't kidnapped . . . I wasn't stolen," Mary-Burden-now-called-Many-Horses replied. "I was a *wablenica,* an orphan. These people . . . saved my life." She was about to go on when her friends called out to her.

"Ota Sunkawakan!" they cried. Without another word, she joined them, turning to wave back at him in a gay and happy way that surprised Tyler. She didn't seem miserable or unhappy at all. How could that be? She was a white person, not Indian.

Ota Sunkawakan. It must mean Many Horses in Sioux. "Many Horses . . . Ota Sunkawakan." Tyler repeated both names again, to fix them in his mind. He stamped his feet to keep them warm and waited impatiently for Isaac to quit playing the fool with One Horn and his cronies.

"Isaac, you ain't going to believe what I just found out!" Tyler exclaimed when he finally got Isaac's attention. "There's someone here just like you and me. I mean, we ain't the only captives Iron Shell's got in camp."

"Ain't seen nobody around here that looks like a white person," Isaac scoffed. "And for sure they ain't no black ones."

"That girl, the tall one we saw the first day we got here—she's white, Isaac. And she speaks English!"

Isaac paused. "You tryin' to fool wit' me, Ty Bohannon? How you know this?"

"She told me, that's how. Her name's Mary Burden, except she's called Many Horses now. She ain't sure how long she's been here, but you know what, Isaac? When the time's right, I bet she'll help us escape. She can even come with us!"

Isaac fixed his glance straight ahead. It was the first time since camp had been moved that Tyler had had a chance to really get down to brass tacks about escaping. It was annoying that the subject still didn't seem to interest Isaac.

"Well, we *got* to get away, Isaac!" Tyler insisted, grabbing Isaac's arm. "We can't stay here. You and me ain't Indians. Mary Burden ain't, either. We got to get back to our own kind. And don't forget we got a score to settle with Captain Little, who—unless you got a short memory—has still got my money, Elway's rifle, not to mention Sooner!"

Isaac remained silent. As they trudged down the hill through the snow, a stark realization dawned on Tyler.

Isaac didn't want to escape.

He was happy in Iron Shell's camp. He liked having One Horn for a friend. He'd found himself a place that he didn't want to leave. Tyler grabbed Isaac's arm again.

"Whoa, Isaac! When we started out ain't you the

one who said it was going to be you for me and me for you? Sure you were! You and me planned to go all the way to Fort Benton, maybe out there to California, where the sun goes down."

Isaac shrugged himself loose of Tyler's grip. "You say *we* got to get back to our own kind," he said in a cool voice. "You be white, Ty. I be black. Your kind ain't exactly my kind. These folks have treated me mighty fair. To them, the color of my skin ain't no-never-mind at all."

Tyler jumped in front of Isaac. "I treated you fair, too, Isaac, don't dare claim I didn't! So'd my mama. I even shared the money Elway paid me, fair and square. Wasn't it me who told you to hide it in your shoe so nobody'd steal it from you? Danged right it was!"

Isaac stubbornly refused to look at him.

"I know why you want to stay, don't I, Isaac?" Tyler said slowly. "Because you're top dog here. Better'n me. And you're wrong about your color not makin' a difference to these folks. It's exactly what makes you special!"

Isaac raised his glance and gave Tyler a hard look. "In the world you an' me lived in back in Missouri, Ty, only white folks was special," Isaac reminded him. "Bein' black meant I was good for workin' like a mule sunup till sundown. Good for livin' in a house with a roof that leaked, to have a daddy that got sold off before I ever knowed him, to have a mama dead before I was knee-high to a grasshopper. In that world, ain't no time

Isaac Peerce was special. It's diff'rent here—and it feel pretty good to me!"

Isaac's black eyes burned with indignation. "Know what your problem is, Ty Bohannon? The shoe's on the other foot now, an' it don't fit worth a doggone, do it? Now you the one who don't count for much, ain't that the Lord's own truth?"

With long strides, Isaac put distance between them, leaving Tyler behind. Isaac was infuriatingly right. The shoe *was* on his foot now, and it hurt worse'n a whupping on a body's bare backside with a green willow switch.

That night Tyler waited in vain for sleep to relieve him of his bitter thoughts. The fire in the center of the tipi grew dim. Finally, the regular breathing of Isaac, Iron Shell, Ooaya, and the twins told him everyone was asleep. As he stared at the shadows dancing on the pale walls of the tipi, Tyler tried to view the matter from Isaac's viewpoint. He could almost understand why Isaac was happy, which made him feel worse.

He shrugged off his blanket and crept noiselessly on hands and knees toward the tipi flap. It might help to sit outside and suck down cold air to clear his heart and head of what was eating him alive. Overhead, a halfmoon scudded through wispy winter clouds. The whole village was silent. Even the rowdy camp dogs were curled snugly in the corners of their owners' tipis. Tyler hugged his knees and gulped deep breaths of frigid air, grateful for the piercing sting of ice crystals in his lungs.

Ooaya had told Isaac that sometimes wolves came skulking around in winter, hoping for an easy meal. Tyler wasn't surprised to see one lingering at the edge of the camp. Mama told stories about wolves, too. Sneaky critters, she called them, always hoping to steal from a homestead what they'd ordinarily have to hunt for in the wild—a few chickens, a new calf, or a colt unlucky enough to be born in winter.

Tyler watched the animal creep closer, weasel-fashion, its belly flat to the ground. It made no sound on the hardpacked snow. It sniffed at the bottom of a tipi, sneaked to another tipi, then another. The critter vanished for a moment, then showed itself again. It was thin, and Tyler felt almost sorry for it. Maybe this one was too old or sick to keep up with its pack anymore and had been left on its own.

The animal eased itself around the edge of the tipi where Many Horses lived. It hesitated in the faint light. Its nose was raised, as if it had caught the scent of something special.

Tyler held his breath. The creature wore a white bib around its neck, as clean as if it'd been freshly washed. Its blue eye glowed in the moonlight like a precious gem.

Ohmygod! Tyler cried silently. Ohmygod, ohmygod!

The animal lowered its belly to the ground, and

Tyler realized that Sooner had picked up his smell. The dog snaked swiftly over the snow, belly flat, making whining noises deep in his throat. When Sooner slid into his arms, Tyler clamped his fingers around the dog's muzzle.

"Not another sound outta you, hear?" he whispered.

Being a stranger in the village, Sooner would be more likely to end up in a stew pot than any dog in camp. As if he understood the danger he was in, Sooner buried his head in Tyler's armpit and was silent.

Oh, if Sooner could talk, what tales he could tell, Tyler thought. About how he'd escaped from Richard Little; how he'd tracked Iron Shell's path all this way; how he'd lived off mice, rabbits, and birds to keep himself alive all these weeks.

Now what? Sooner couldn't be turned away. Yet there was still snow on the ground; Tyler knew there was no way for them to escape together tonight. Meantime, how could Sooner be kept safe?

There wasn't any way, Tyler knew.

He squared his jaw, grateful for the sweet feel of Sooner's thin, warm body snuggled against his own. All right; he wouldn't try to keep him a secret. Tomorrow, he'd get Isaac to help convince Iron Shell and Ooaya the dog would be an asset, not a liability.

Tyler's glance fell on the tipi where Many Horses slept. He'd ask her to help, too. He'd tell her the whole story—how he left home because Mama got married again, all about Bigger and how he died, what happened with Captain Little—everything.

He lifted the tipi flap and beckoned Sooner inside. He folded the dog inside his blanket and curled his body around Sooner's. He put his arm around the dog and laid his hand against Sooner's chest, where he could feel the dog's heart beat steadily against his palm.

The hatefulness of the last few weeks vanished. The quarrel with Isaac was forgotten. With a deep sigh, Tyler slept better than he had since Captain Little said, "Go along with Iron Shell, and don't raise a fuss about it."

Chapter Eleven

Ooaya's rosy-brown face turned black as a thunderhead when she woke to find a strange dog in her tipi.

On the coldest nights she went to sleep partly dressed, so when she leaped out of bed, she was ready to do battle. She seized a butcher knife from its special place atop one of her *parfleches* and honed it briskly against her leather-clad thigh to put an edge on its gleaming blade. She fixed Sooner with a menacing glare as he lay curled in the cradle of Tyler's arms.

With her toe she roused Isaac to help dispatch the intruder. Dazed by the racket she made, Tyler clutched Sooner even tighter. Ooaya might kill the dog—but she'd have to chop him into pieces first.

From her gestures, Tyler could see that Ooaya was telling Isaac there already were too many dogs in the village. One more meant another greedy thief skulking about that would raid the racks of drying meat when the weather got warm. With a slashing motion she demonstrated that she intended to put the intruder in a stew pot this very morning.

Isaac scrambled out of bed, as startled as Ooaya was to see the red dog nestled in Tyler's arms. He wasted no time answering Ooaya with rapid motions and words even louder than hers.

Before his eyes, Tyler saw a reenactment of Bigger's death. (He'd told Isaac about it so often that Isaac plainly believed he'd witnessed the event himself.) Next, how Sooner helped save the family back in Sweet Creek from being robbed by scalawags. Last, how Sooner must have escaped from Captain Little by jumping overboard, how he'd finally tracked Tyler to this very tipi.

Ooaya listened, one hand braced on her hip, the knife resting flat against her thigh. Her expression softened as Isaac rattled on. Not much, but a little. At last, she shrugged her shoulders and put the knife back in its place. She poked the embers of the fire to life, grumbling and throwing dark looks in Sooner's direction. Soon the tipi was filled with the fragrant smell of *wicagnaska*, or dried gooseberries, as she stirred up a pot of breakfast mush.

"Did you tell her what I hope you did? That no way can she kill Sooner?" Tyler asked Isaac. "Before she puts him in any pot she'll have to put me in first, on account of I'll fight for him to my last breath."

"Don't go gettin' yourself in a lather," Isaac soothed. "I've cooled her down, at least for now. Ooaya's not as bad as you think, Ty. A person just has to know how to talk to her."

"And you do, right?" Tyler shot back as he jumped up and shook out his blanket. In her way, Ooaya was as fussy as Mama about housekeeping chores, and putting sleeping gear away each morning was one of them. As he held the blanket against the glow of the morning fire, Tyler saw for the first time how pitifully thin it was.

He frowned as he watched Isaac fold up his own sleeping robe—the rich, warm buffalo robe Ooaya had so generously given him. When Isaac knelt to stroke Sooner's ears, the dog nuzzled Isaac and covered his face with slobbery doggie kisses. The red fool! Tyler's heart felt pinched to realize Sooner thought Isaac was as special as everyone else did.

"Listen, don't be peeved wit' me," Isaac advised gently. "The way you be feelin' now—you know, shoved aside like you didn't count for much—that's how I lived most of my life, Ty. Everybody had rights but me. Just the same, I wouldn't a wished any of this on you for nothin', you know that."

Tyler sighed. Jealousy leaked out of him one sour drop at a time. "Oh, I know none of it's your fault, Isaac," he said. Without waiting for Ooaya to holler at him, Tyler reached through the tipi flap to fetch extra wood from the pile he'd stacked up yesterday. At least she didn't whack him on the head anymore if she heard him talking to Isaac.

"But didn't it make you mad, Isaac, bein' treated so bad? So mad, you wanted to chuck it all and run off?" Tyler asked. "Didn't you ever think you'd as soon be dead as be somebody's slave one more day?" Because that's exactly how he felt himself each morning when Isaac traipsed off with One Horn and the others to play *hotanacute*, ice hockey, or throw a *shoshiman*, a snow-snake, across the ice on the frozen creek.

"For certain," Isaac admitted. "But where could I run to?" A faraway look came into his eyes as he reflected on his past. "First time I met you, Ty, I'd never even had a pair of shoes! You gave me the first boots I ever owned, remember? Handsome yeller leather they was, with rawhide laces long enough to go twice around my shins." Isaac smiled as he recalled the thrill of that gift.

"But no matter how bad things got," Isaac went on, "I was always glad to see the sun come up in the mornin'. Never once did I figger Isaac Peerce'd be better off dead. Don't you go thinkin' that way, either. Reckon your daddy would tell you the same thing."

The mention of Papa caused a familiar, bruised feeling in the middle of Tyler's chest. As Ooaya continued to stir the pot of gooseberry mush, Tyler decided this would be as good a time as any to talk to Isaac again about trying to escape.

"Yesterday, you didn't want to talk about making

plans to get away from here, Isaac," he whispered. "But they can't be put off forever. We got to figure out the hows, whens, and whys of escaping. Not that we can run away tomorrow, mind you. But if we're ready to light out soon as the weather breaks . . ."

Tyler let his words trail off. Back home, he could go wherever he wanted, whenever he wanted. He'd never had to think about what freedom meant. Now, he was obsessed by the wish to get it back.

"Din't you hear what I just tol' you?" Isaac said, giving Sooner a final belly scratching. "It's like when you talked about gettin' away from Captain Little—you said there was no place to escape *to*. It's the same now, Ty. We got no rifle, no map, no way to make a fire. In fact, we got no idea in the whole wide world exactly where we is."

Tyler turned away. In his usually savvy way, Isaac was right. When someone owned you—like the Sioux owned him and Isaac now—a person's options were mighty few. Since Isaac had lived that way once, maybe he could live that way again. But Tyler knew that Black Jack Bohannon's son couldn't. Wouldn't.

When the morning meal was finished (Tyler made sure Sooner got a portion of mush when Ooaya wasn't looking), Tyler put on his thin buckskin shirt and ratty scarf and went outside. He took a leather sling that made it easier to gather one or two good-sized bunches of wood rather than make a half-dozen trips back and forth carrying it by the armload.

Isaac headed for One Horn's tipi, which meant Sooner was torn between who to follow.

"You best come with me," Tyler told him. Sooner might as well get out of the habit of keeping company with Isaac, especially since it was clear the three of them wouldn't be escaping together. Anyway, there was a flock of dogs of all shapes, colors, and sizes always hanging around One Horn's tipi.

If Sooner got ganged up on—and being a newcomer in camp, he surely would be—and if the pack of dogs were led by that tall, mud-colored mutt that was One Horn's favorite, he'd have a hard time defending himself. Isaac said One Horn named that dog Hoka, or Badger, because more than once he'd fought another dog to the death, the way badgers handled their enemies.

Side by side, Sooner and Tyler headed for the woods and the nearby creek. Ahead, Tyler could hear the voices of One Horn and his cronies who were already deep in the forest. He'd seen them take rabbit sticks with them—short sticks, sharp as daggers on one end, weighted slightly at the opposite end—that were thrown at a rabbit like a spear.

Tyler closed his ears to the sound of their good-natured hoots. Joyful banter like that was another reminder that he was excluded from the play of boys.

Women's work—how Tyler hated the sound of those

two words! To him fell the chore of doing what Ooaya herself would have to do if she hadn't picked him to be a daughter. To Isaac—Isaac, who was everyone's favorite—fell the chance to hunt rabbits, shoot squirrels with a bow and arrow, or play games.

Before he started to gather wood, Tyler chopped a hole in the creek ice. The heavy mallet he used had a head made of a sharp stone fastened to a stout oak handle with a shrink-dried wrapping of rawhide. The minute the hole was open, Sooner stuck his muzzle down and drank his fill. When he finished stacking wood, Tyler planned to fill Ooaya's two buffalo-stomach pouches with as much water as he could carry back to camp. With a sigh, he spread the leather sling flat on the snow and began to pile sticks and heavier branches on it.

For days afterward, Tyler tried to reconstruct in his mind the events that followed.

He remembered hearing the distant cries of One Horn's gang mingled with the barking of their dogs as he stacked wood. His thirst quenched, Sooner had stretched himself out on the creek bank, head on his paws, and sleepily followed the wood-gathering process.

The sling held nearly a full load when Tyler realized he could no longer hear the sound of dogs. When their cries came again, they seemed closer. *Much closer.* Their howling wasn't playful anymore. A crazed sound filled their yelps.

A thrill of fear warmed Tyler down to the tips of his

freezing fingers, as he understood what it meant. Badger and the other dogs had been downwind of Sooner. They'd just picked up the scent of a stranger in their territory, and it had filled them with an appetite for murder.

Before he could grab the wood sling, yell to Sooner, and dash back to camp, the dogs—seven abreast, with Badger out in front—burst through the screen of leafless alders, willows, and cottonwoods along the opposite edge of the creek. Sooner raised his red head, his ears pricked sharply forward. The heavy hair on the back of his neck lifted stiffly. His pale eye was the color of ice, the brown one filled with fire as he watched the assassins charge across the frozen surface of the creek bed.

Badger was the first to lay into Sooner. The other dogs—spotted ones, black ones, skinny scrappy ones hardly worth throwing in anybody's pot, even one with the baying cry of a hound—circled round and round. Their tongues hung out of their mouths, foamy with slaver. Their eyes were red with bloodlust as they waited for a chance to take a chunk out of Sooner's hide themselves.

Swiftly, Tyler reached into the pile of wood beside him and seized a stout branch in either hand. He flailed away at the circle of dogs that kept Sooner pinned against the ice-covered creek bank. He hit each dog as hard as he could. He didn't care if he split their heads wide open, if each blow sounded as hollow as that of a smashed melon. Too bad if brains got splattered across the snow in scarlet gobs. He had no pity for murderers.

But there was no way to get in close enough to take a whack at Badger. The only thing Tyler could do was hold the six other killers at bay. It's your fight now, Sooner, he thought. You're the only one who can save you.

Badger was long in the leg, had the large, blunt head of a mastiff, and a pair of jaws that looked as if they could crack a buffalo shin bone in half with a single crunch.

By contrast, Sooner had the pointed muzzle and narrow jaw of his Scottish ancestors. His greatest advantage came from those forebears who'd herded countless generations of sheep along the windswept Highlands. They'd been bred to be as nimble on their feet as foxes, and Sooner had inherited their agility.

Each time Badger made a lunge in his direction, Sooner suddenly wasn't there. He'd already leaped a foot or two to one side or the other. Like his sheepherding ancestors, he kept his belly flat to the ground, enabling him to come up under Badger and nip his underparts before Badger could whirl and nip him in return.

If Badger ever clamped down with those grizzly-bear jaws, though, Tyler knew it would all be over for Sooner. Once Badger got Sooner down, the other dogs would move in for the kill and would rip him to bloody shreds.

As he took a wild swing at a spotted cur that tried to enter the fray from the side, Tyler realized the dogs' racket had attracted Isaac, One Horn, and the others, who had gathered on the far creek bank.

Then it happened.

Badger made a pass at Sooner's jugular but missed. His gaping jaws angled harmlessly off the mark, slid down Sooner's thickly furred shoulder, then clamped Sooner's upper left foreleg. The red dog let out a shrill, wild cry of agony. He twisted first one way, then the other to free himself. Tyler saw the fur and flesh peel away from Sooner's leg as neatly as rind from an orange.

In moments, the snow inside the circle where the two dogs battled was dyed red. Sooner and Badger tumbled down the icy bank onto the slick surface of the frozen creek, trailing crimson ribbons behind them. An awful sense of doom swept over Tyler. This death would be far worse than Bigger's, who had died swiftly and cleanly from a single bullet hole in the chest. Sooner would be torn to pieces by this insane mob and would die one bloody inch at a time.

What accounted for what happened next? Was there an ancient memory buried deep in Sooner's brain, one inherited from a wily great-great-grandparent who'd battled a Highland wolf in a setting like this one?

Sooner, wounded and bleeding but still nimble and weasel-like, maneuvered Badger across the ice toward the dark hole Tyler had chopped to get water for Ooaya. Badger, heavier and less nimble, fell through first. Even so, true to his name, the mud-colored mutt never let go of his victim's leg.

Sooner was pulled into the water along with Badger. Tyler hurled himself belly-first across the ice, seized

Sooner around the hind quarters, and held on. Badger's dark muzzle was only inches away, and Tyler could see that the dog's fiendish, red-rimmed eyes were filled with rage. He'll hang on till he drowns, Tyler realized. In the process, Sooner would drown, too.

Slowly, Badger's weight and his death-grip dragged Sooner deeper into the hole. The black water rose to his neck. Tyler braced himself on the slick ice as best he could, struggling to keep Sooner's muzzle above the water level.

Badger's head now was totally submerged. Bubbles rose from his nostrils and broke on the surface. Yet he held on, eyes wide open and fixed on his enemy. Only when his lungs finally filled with water did Badger's jaws release their hold on Sooner's leg—not slowly, but with a sudden snap, as if a spring had broken.

Tyler hauled Sooner backward across the ice and squeezed him hard around the middle, expelling a gush of water from the red dog's mouth. Without their leader, the other killers milled around, sniffing and whining, the fire gone out of their lust for mayhem.

Until that moment, all had been silent on the far creek bank. Now One Horn leaped forward with a cry of disbelief and plunged both arms into the hole, searching for Badger. But Badger's body had already slipped away and was being carried downstream beneath the ice. It wouldn't be seen again until the spring thaw came.

Tyler stared down at Sooner. The exposed bone in

his foreleg gleamed with a pearly sheen. The water on the thick hair of his white bib turned to frozen needles in the cold air. His fiery brown eye was closed. The pale one was open, the color of the ice where he lay. It stared across a landscape that only the dying dog himself could see.

Tyler felt Isaac at his side. "Let me he'p you haul him back to camp," he said.

With a single swift movement, Isaac cleared the leather sling of its load of wood and helped lift Sooner onto it. Wordlessly, they headed back to Ooaya's tipi. Tyler couldn't have shed a tear if he'd been ordered to, but a grisly thought occurred to him. Ooaya might get her wish. Maybe there'd be dog stew on today's menu after all.

CHAPTER TWELVE

C'aske and Hepa—Isaac said the twins' names meant "first to be born" and "second to be born"—looked up from their bowls of gooseberry mush. Their round black eyes were as curious as their mother's when Isaac and Tyler hauled the wood sling into the tipi. Ooaya peered down to see what they were carrying.

"*T'aka tu, t'aka tu!*" she screeched when she saw what it was. "Outside, outside!" She swept the air with both arms to brush all three of them back out into the cold, bright morning.

Isaac silenced her in the middle of a screech. He explained that Sooner was badly wounded and probably dying. Ooaya wasn't impressed. To her, a dog was a dog. Its best place was in a stew pot, not upsetting the order of her household.

"*T'aka tu!*" she shouted again, and when Tyler and

Isaac didn't move quickly enough she snatched up her butcher knife. She demonstrated that she knew one way to end the discussion permanently.

"Sometimes there just ain't no way to reason with her!" Isaac growled. There was nothing to do but carry Sooner back through the tipi flap into the freezing air.

Across the way, Ooaya's shouts attracted the attention of Many Horses. "What happened?" she called. "Why is Ooaya so angry?" Grief stopped Tyler's reply in his throat, so she came closer to find out for herself.

"Ooaya won't let us take care of him in her tipi," he said matter-of-factly. "Reckon it's too late anyhow. Badger's already dead. Sooner can't be far behind."

"But look!" Many Horses exclaimed, pointing at the motionless red form in the sling. "I just saw his ribs move! He's still breathing!" Since she'd spoken to him that first time on the sledding hill, Many Horses's English had gotten better each day. It was as if, given a chance to use her native tongue again, words she'd known long ago rushed back to her like a creek at floodtime.

"I will ask my mother if she can help," Many Horses offered. "Brown Shawl Woman is respected by everyone for her good medicine. She will tell me what to put on your dog's leg." She dashed back to her own tipi, disappeared behind its flap, then emerged a few minutes later with something cupped in the palm of her right hand.

"Brown Shawl Woman says this poultice will work." She flashed Tyler an apologetic glance. "I asked if we could bring him into our tipi, but she said she could not create bad feelings between herself and an old friend like Ooaya."

Tyler looked down at what Many Horses held. A poultice? It was a glistening, dark, moist wad on a piece of deerskin. In the other hand she carried several large dry oak leaves.

"What is it?" Tyler asked. He hated to think so, but it looked suspiciously like a fresh dog dropping.

"Brown Shawl Woman makes it from puffballs she collects in the woods," Many Horses answered. "She dries them, crushes them, then adds the root of yellow pond lilies. She binds the mixture together with pitch from a balsam tree. She said it stops bleeding and will draw the edges of a wound together so it heals properly. If Wakan Tanka wishes the dog to recover, he will."

"Wakan Tanka?"

"The Great Spirit," Many Horses replied, and ducked her head shyly.

Isaac helped Tyler lower Sooner's sling onto the snow. Many Horses carefully smoothed the poultice into the gaping wound on the dog's leg. Next, she placed the oak leaves in layers over the poultice, wrapped the piece of deerskin around the leg, and tied everything in place with a narrow strip of leather. Through it all, Sooner lay as if dead. Many Horses claimed she'd seen him breathing, but Tyler couldn't detect it himself.

Toward evening, when the winter shadows turned

blue and bitter, Tyler ate the thick soup Isaac carried out to him. He smiled weakly. At least it wasn't dog soup. Not yet, anyway.

He left a portion for Sooner, and tried to poke a scrap of meat into the side of the dog's mouth. The taste didn't rouse him; the meat fell out onto the leather sling. Sooner's nose was dry, so Tyler moistened the end of his scarf with spit to dampen it. Still, there was no response. Instead, Tyler noticed the dog's lips were pulled back from his long incisors in a death snarl.

Without being asked, Isaac returned to the creek and collected all the wood Tyler had gathered. He fetched it back by the armload and stacked it next to the entrance of the tipi. Tyler took a few sticks from the pile and laid them for a fire while Isaac got a hot coal from Ooaya's fire inside.

"*Heyoka, heyoka!*" Tyler heard her exclaim. He grimaced. The words probably meant "Fool, fool!"

Isaac also brought back evergreen boughs. He helped Tyler make a bed on top of the leather sling so that Sooner's body could be raised off the frozen ground. Tyler dragged the bed, with Sooner on it, as close to the blaze of the fire as was safe. He propped his threadbare blanket up on sticks to make a three-sided tent, the better to trap warmth from the flames.

The softness of the boughs tempted Tyler to lie down himself. He was numb with fatigue, but forced himself to doze sitting up. He couldn't risk going to sleep and letting the fire go out. Worse, in the dark One Horn might try to avenge Badger's death by finishing Sooner off himself.

"I'll keep you company," Isaac suggested. He hunkered down on the opposite side of the fire, his knees tucked under his chin, his fur-trimmed cap pulled low.

"Sooner don't need both of us," Tyler murmured. "I just want to be right here in case—"

He didn't finish. In case he dies, he almost said. He'd been with Bigger the day that a pistol wound bloomed like a rose on his white bib. The least he could do now was be present at the moment Bigger's son died. But if he didn't say *die* out loud, maybe it wouldn't happen. With luck, the concoction of dried puffballs, lily roots, and pitch might work.

The night air was fiercely cold. Overhead, a half-moon was glued like a broken white plate in the black sky. The three stars in Orion's belt—Mr. Blackburn said they were named Mintaka, Alnitam, and Alnitah—glittered like precious jewels.

Fitful thoughts passed through Tyler's mind as he dozed. The cabin at Sweet Creek would be so warm right now. . . . How safe his life had been back then. . . . Then, to put iron in his backbone, Tyler reminded himself that nobody drove him away with a stick. He'd chosen this journey of his own free will. Just the same, Sooner wouldn't be dying if Captain Richard Little hadn't betrayed him and Isaac.

Betrayed!

The word brought Tyler wide awake. He glanced down at the red dog lying against the curve of his crossed knees, and felt the blood in his veins congeal. In the firelight, Sooner's body was as rigid as if it were already frozen. Tyler lowered his cheek to Sooner's rib cage. Did he hear the faint tick of the dog's heart beneath his thick red coat? Or was it only the snap of burning wood from the fire?

"If Sooner dies," Tyler vowed, his words hanging in round white puffs on the dark air (there, he'd said the word out loud), "I swear on his poor red carcass that Captain Little will pay double for what he's done."

By morning, Sooner was able to feebly lift up his head an inch. Tyler dripped water onto his tongue, moistened his nose, and pushed bits of mush into his mouth. This time, Sooner accepted the offering.

Tyler kept the fire going all day beside Ooaya's tipi, on into the next night and several nights thereafter. Isaac stuck close and never traipsed off with One Horn anymore. Instead, he took over the job of carrying water for Ooaya and making sure she had enough wood.

Tyler suspected it was Isaac's presence that kept One Horn and his cronies at a distance. Now that it was Isaac who did the work of a woman, though, One Horn and the others never cupped their hands around their mouths and hollered, "Ho, woman worker!"

Six days after his ordeal, Sooner could stand for a few minutes each morning. He put no weight on his left leg, nor could he take a step. Slowly, his brown eye recovered a hint of its familiar warm glow. The pale one remained as cold and hard as the ice where the battle with Badger had taken place.

Many Horses came every day to see how her mother's poultice was working. "Brown Shawl Woman says on the seventh morning you must remove it," she advised. She helped Tyler loosen the rawhide bandage, then peeled the leaves aside. She carefully lifted the dark brown poultice away from Sooner's wound. "Look!" she exclaimed.

To Tyler's amazement, there was no sign of pearly bone. Instead, a thin layer of fresh pink tissue covered it. Best of all, the edges of the wound were already shrinking together.

"*Ho hecetu!*" Many Horses exclaimed, pleased. "*Ho hecetu!*"

"Aw, talk English," Tyler begged. "Otherwise I don't know what the heck you mean!"

"I said, 'It is good!'—and it is," Many Horses said. "Say it after me; it will help you learn my language."

"*Ho hecetu,*" Tyler mumbled, but only to please her. The words tasted foreign on his tongue.

"My language," Many Horses had said. She'd lived with the Sioux so long, she didn't think of English as her own anymore. She didn't speak of God, either, like a regular white person. Instead, she prayed to someone named Wakan Tanka.

"Brown Shawl Woman says the muscle will never

come back entirely," Many Horses said as she inspected Sooner's wound. "She says the leg will always be a little weak, and when the hair grows back it will be white."

As she knelt beside Sooner, Tyler studied Many Horses as if seeing her for the first time. Everything about her—her clothes, her long dark braids, the darkness of her complexion from long days spent out of doors—spelled only one word: I-n-d-i-a-n. Did that mean she'd say no when he asked her to help him get away from camp as soon as Sooner was ready to travel?

Rather than approach the subject head-on, Tyler decided to talk around it in a circle. Isaac wasn't the only one—maybe not even the best one—to talk to about escaping.

"Do you have a horse of your own?" Tyler asked casually, as if the answer were of no special importance.

Many Horses seemed surprised. "Of course," she answered, then added with a smile, "though not as many as my name implies. I have only two. One is a fine bay mare with four white feet who will have her first colt in the spring. The other is a handsome spotted pony that I ride when we meet our relatives every summer at the Place Where the Hills Are Black. I wear my doeskin dress, too, because Brown Shawl Woman wishes me to make a fine impression."

She frowned at Tyler, almost as if she could read his mind. "I was given a horse almost as soon as I came to live here, because no one was afraid I would run away," she pointed out. "You see, Iron Shell gave me to Brown

Shawl Woman, who then had the right to decide my fate. She could have given me away as a slave, or even ordered that I be killed. Instead, she took me into her tipi and treated me as her daughter."

Many Horses raised her brows. "Of course, captives like you and Isaac aren't allowed to have horses. It would be too dangerous."

"Dangerous? We don't aim to hurt nobody," Tyler objected.

"Iron Shell knows you'd try to run away," Many Horses retorted.

"Didn't *you* ever want to?" Tyler shot back. It was almost the same question he'd put to Isaac about being a slave. If a person wasn't really an Indian—and Many Horses surely wasn't—why did she want to stay here? She waited hand and foot on her adopted mother, so wasn't her life almost the same as a slave's?

Many Horses let her glance slide past his and didn't answer. Tyler wondered if she was thinking of the family she'd lost. Or worse, how they'd been lost. "It's time for me to help Brown Shawl Woman," she said, as if she regretted saying so much. Before Tyler could say another word, Many Horses vanished inside her adopted mother's tipi.

Tyler turned back to Sooner. He fondled the dog's ears, wishing his discussion with Many Horses had ended on a different note. One thing was plain: He'd have to know her a lot better before it'd be safe to ask her to help him get a horse. If he spoke too soon—without knowing what was truly in her heart—she might feel obliged to tell Brown Shawl Woman, who then would tell Ooaya, who in less than a heartbeat would report the matter to Iron Shell. Tyler shuddered to think what would happen then.

It made Tyler feel peculiar to know there was no one—*no one at all*—he could turn to. Isaac had all but admitted he didn't want to escape. Many Horses had forgotten she was white. That left only one person in this whole wild country he could trust: himself.

By the time Sooner could bear weight on his leg and walk a few steps, the winter snow melted, becoming scattered islands of white in widening seas of green. Tender new grass came up all across the prairie. One by one, the big-bellied mares in Iron Shell's pony herd dropped their colts, including the white-footed bay mare that belonged to Many Horses. An hour after birth the colts staggered around on stiltlike legs, their eyes wet and full of wonder. Within an hour they were poking at their mothers' underbellies for a teat and sucked lustily, stirring the air in circles with their bushy tails. By the second day they were able to gallop at their mothers' sides.

One Horn and his friends doffed their jackets for lighter clothes as the weather warmed. Tyler's hands, which were so badly chapped, the skin on his knuckles and around his fingernails had cracked and bled—began to heal. Ooaya's mood turned almost genial; she even allowed Sooner into her tipi. Nearby, Brown Shawl Woman crept out every afternoon to sit in the mild air, her wrinkled brown face turned up to the warmth of the sun.

Tyler wondered if the change of season might mean that Many Horses would be easier to ask about getting a horse. When he saw her doing needlework with her mother one afternoon, he decided to find out.

"You said you had two horses," Tyler reminded her. He spoke without worrying that Brown Shawl Woman would report what he said. She spoke no English and wouldn't be able to follow their conversation.

"Maybe we could go riding sometime," he suggested. If they could get off by themselves, away from camp with its watching eyes and listening ears, he could lay out a plan to Many Horses about helping him get away.

To his amazement, Many Horses turned scarlet and pressed her hand to her mouth. "My mother would never permit such a thing!" she exclaimed, flashing a glance in Brown Shawl Woman's direction.

"She is NOT your mother!" Tyler wanted to shout. Instead, he clenched his teeth and muttered, "You told me your family's name was Burden. If you remember that much about being a white person, why do you call Brown Shawl woman *mother*? Besides, what's so terrible about you and me goin' riding together?"

The suggestion had seemed simple enough. If he'd decided to walk Sallyjo McCarthy down the road to her folks' place after school (he never had, of course, because she was too giddy and gossipy), it might've set his classmates' tongues to wagging—Oat Snepp's most of all—but there wasn't a law against it.

"You're not one of the People," Many Horses murmured. "When I marry, it will be to someone from one of the Otchenti Chakowin, the Seven Council Fires."

Tyler was exasperated. "Marry? Who said anything about getting married?" The idea was outlandish. "How can you talk about getting married, for lordy sakes? You aren't one of the People any more'n I am!" he exclaimed hotly. "Your name's Mary Burden. You're as white as me!"

Many Horses dropped her glance and examined the piece of beaded deerskin in her lap as if it held a secret message. When she looked at him again, Tyler noticed her bright gaze was cloudy.

"I hardly remember anything about being white," she said softly. "Only that when I was very little we lived in a place called, um, it was a name that made me think of an evil spirit. You know—what do you call it—a witch? Yes, it was a name that sounded like *witch* . . . but it's been so long ago, I can't remember."

"You mean Wichita?" Tyler prompted. Many Horses nodded, her eyes wide with surprise.

"Wi-chi-ta." She rolled the name on her tongue as if

it were a flavor she hadn't tasted in a long while. "Yes, once we lived in a place called Wichita. . . ."

"Why, that's in Kansas! Right next door to Missouri, where I come from!" Tyler blurted. "If you remember that much, we could track down the rest of your kinfolk, your aunts and uncles and cousins and such. You're the only survivor in your family—I bet they'd be mighty glad to get you back," he said.

With her fingertip, Many Horses traced the beaded design she was making. Tyler noticed that her nails were broken and rimmed with dirt. Her thick dark braids gleamed with the oil Brown Shawl Woman smoothed on them when she plaited them every morning. The first thing Mary Burden's relatives would do when she showed up in Wichita would be to stick her in a tub filled with hot, soapy water and give her a good scrubbing!

Tyler tried to understand what bothered Many Horses. Of course, to leave the only safety she'd known since she'd become an orphan would be hard. Before he could stop himself, Tyler asked the question he'd wondered about since the first day she'd told him her white-girl's name.

"How'd it happen?" he asked. "I mean, you getting to be a *wablenica*?" Maybe she would explain how a person could come to love the people who'd done such a terrible thing—killing her parents, maybe even scalping them. He tried to imagine Mama, Lucas, Rosa Lee being lost that way, never to be seen again. He couldn't.

"I'm not sure," Many Horses answered. "But it wasn't the People who fell upon us that day. It was the *hohes*, the Crows, who are our enemies. All I remember" —she paused and fixed her gaze in the middle distance, as if she could see the scene all over again—"are the sounds the *hohes* made as they rode down on us."

She hesitated, as if looking at an album of old pictures and trying to remember the scenes and the people in them. "My mother told me to take my brother back to the river we'd just crossed. 'Hide there,' she said. 'I'll come back to get you.' My brother—I think his name was Willy—was only a baby. He wiggled away from me and fell into the water. Before I could catch him, he was carried away." Many Horses's words trailed off.

"When I couldn't hear the *hohes* anymore, I searched for Willy again. I couldn't find him anywhere. I waited for my mother to come, then I went back to the wagon—" Many Horses stopped and sighed deeply.

"You went back to the wagon—" Tyler prompted.

"A long time later, Iron Shell and his people found me. Brown Shawl Woman says I was the only one alive. All the rest were dead—my parents, my uncle and his wife, my grandfather. The wagon was empty. Everything had been stolen by the *hohes*."

"How long ago was that?"

"I don't know," Many Horses admitted. "In the beginning, I kept a little stick and made notches in the bark to count the days. After a while, I forgot to make the marks. Finally, I threw the stick away. It didn't matter anymore."

It was your life you threw away, Tyler wanted to remind her. The look on Many Horses's smooth, dark face silenced him, but the terrible story she told convinced him he'd been right when he'd told Isaac that Many Horses must come with them. The reason she'd stayed here was because there was no way to leave, no one to encourage her. It was his bounden duty to help her.

So what if Isaac didn't want to go? Many Horses deserved a chance to be Mary Burden again.

CHAPTER THIRTEEN

Three weeks later, Iron Shell's camp was struck so swiftly that Tyler knew something big was up. The story Many Horses told about being orphaned in an attack from the Crows was fresh in his mind, making his heart thonk with dread. Did the sudden move mean *hohes* were headed this way?

"What's going on, Isaac?" Tyler asked. Isaac, with his connections to One Horn, usually heard the latest news even quicker than Iron Shell.

"Tell you later, when we got more time to talk," Isaac answered.

Tyler helped Ooaya dismantle the tipi and load her *parfleches* on the travois. Her other paraphernalia was added, including enough sticks of wood to build a fire right away at the new camp. As soon as C'aske and Hepa were lifted atop the pile of possessions behind Ooaya's pony, the trip commenced.

Sooner limped along beside Tyler, favoring his right leg. As Brown Shawl Woman had predicted, the hair came in white over his healed wound. It looked as if a piece had been cut off the white bib on his chest and tied there.

"All right, now it's later," Tyler prompted Isaac as they walked beside Ooaya's travois. Although the camp had been dismantled in haste, Tyler noticed that everyone was merrier than he'd ever seen them. He seemed to be the only one who was scared. "So what's happening, Isaac?"

"We be headed to a big gathering out yonder at one of the forts. Some men are comin' from far away to talk to the tribes about a treaty." Isaac sounded as lighthearted as the others were acting.

"White folks want Indians to stay in one place, inside the boundaries of somethin' called a reservation. Settlers don't want red folks wanderin' all over the prairie anymore. One Horn says the Seven Council Fires will meet first to decide if they'll go live at this new place like the whites want 'em to."

Many Horses had mentioned the Seven Council Fires, too. Tyler wished he'd asked her more about them.

"See, the Sioux are made of up seven tribes," Isaac explained. "Iron Shell's folks belong to the biggest one. They call themselves the Oglalas, which means 'scatter one's own.' The other tribes are the Brules, the Miniconjous, the Two Kettles, the Sans Arcs, the Hunkpapas, and the Sihasapa."

Tyler gritted his teeth. "Next time I need a history lesson, reckon I'll know who to come to," he grumbled.

Isaac paid him no mind. "Anyway, that's where we're headed. Up yonder to a place called Fort Laramie, to listen to what the white men have to say. One Horn's glad, on account of he's got kin that belong to the Two Kettles tribe, and now he'll get to see 'em again."

Tyler was silent. A sudden coolness swept over him. "Captain Little said I could be ransomed for money, remember?" he reminded Isaac. "If white folks are at this meeting, Iron Shell will be tempted to trade me off."

Isaac shrugged. "Oh, I reckon he's forgot about that by now."

"I don't think he forgets *anything*," Tyler countered. "If you and me don't aim to be split up for keeps, Isaac, we better figure out a way to make a run for it before this trip gets too far along. I got a feeling it's now or never."

"Oh, it'll be a long time before we get where we're goin'," Isaac assured him, and kept his gaze fastened straight ahead. Obviously, the subject of escaping still didn't interest him. "We don't need to get all fussed up about makin' plans yet."

"Maybe you don't—but I do," Tyler pointed out. "As sure as my name's Tyler Bohannon, Iron Shell will trade me off for money. That ain't the worst part, either."

Isaac pretended not to hear.

"Once I get traded, those white folks might get the idea I'm not growed up enough to be out here on my own," Tyler went on. "They'll ship me back to Missouri quick as you please—without any money and worse, without Elway's Winchester. No way do I aim for that to happen, Isaac. Besides, I still got a debt to settle with Captain Little."

Isaac scuffed at the ground as they walked along. He wore Indian mocassins now, a pair One Horn had given him, decorated with blue-and-yellow beadwork. "I learned a long time ago it don't pay to hold grudges, Ty," he said quietly. "If you calculate everything accordin' to when and where and how you can get even, you turn yourself into a prisoner. I coulda done that myself—but I din't."

"After everything that's happened—Sooner getting practically killed, me stuck doing woman's work from sunup till sundown—you still want to stay here, don't you, Isaac?" Tyler said.

Isaac continued to stare straight ahead.

Tyler stopped in his tracks. "Captain Little sold me out, now you're fixin' to do the same thing, ain't you, Isaac?" Now that it was put into words, Tyler wasn't as surprised by the discovery as he thought he'd be. Sold out. Betrayed. Meant the same thing, didn't they? The words clanged loudly inside his head.

Papa did it when he went off to Texas.

Mama did it when she married Elway Snepp.

Captain Little did it after the Indian brave was killed. Isaac planned to do the same.

Fine. Isaac didn't want to leave? Forget him, then. Tyler would rather cut out his own tongue before he ever mentioned the subject again.

The next morning Tyler saw Iron Shell draw Isaac aside and tell him something that caused a broad smile to brighten his scarred black face. Tyler almost smiled himself when he heard what Isaac had to report.

"He says he's goin' to give us horses, Ty! We ain't goin' to have to go a-foot no more. Iron Shell wants to get to Fort Laramie as quick as he can, but you and me slow things down too much by walkin' along so pokey."

Two fresh horses were fetched from the herd, but neither was fitted with a bridle. Instead, a rawhide rope was looped around the neck of each one. Ooaya fastened the ropes over the tall horn of her Indian saddle and led the mounts close on either side of her own pony.

It struck Tyler as humiliating to be led along like a careless child. Just the same, it was good to be mounted, to be able to look across the prairie, so pale and green with its new covering of grass, with flowers scattered here and there in bright patches of red, yellow, and blue.

He sighed, though, when he saw the horse Isaac had been given. It was much larger than his own, built for speed and endurance, with long, straight legs. It was cinnamon-colored, covered nose to tail with white spots the size of a man's fist, as handsome a horse as anybody could wish for. No surprise! Once again, Isaac got the best.

By the time the sun dropped to the horizon and camp was made the second night, however, Tyler had grown genuinely fond of the small, plain pony he'd been given. It was a sturdy little beast, about the same soft gray color as a mouse.

"We call that color *hota*," Many Horses told Tyler. "Some say gray horses like that one came to us long ago from people in the country Where Snow Never Falls."

"You mean Mexico?" Tyler asked. Papa said in one of his final letters that it hardly ever snowed down there, and that he'd have welcomed the sight of a clean blanket of white to cover the parched, brown earth of the desert.

"Perhaps," Many Horses answered, holding her hand over her mouth to silence a giggle. "You whites give names to places that make no sense to us. We call places by what they mean—like Many Trees Near Red Mountain, which is one of our favorite campgrounds."

Tyler smiled, remembering the mouse Lucas kept as a pet up in the sleeping loft till Mama found out about it.

"Well, to me he's the color of a mouse, so that's what I'm going to call him—Mouse," he said, glancing at the horse staked nearby. Iron Shell kept them close so that no time would be wasted sorting them out of the larger pony herd every morning. The sight of the little gray horse caused a feeling almost like happiness to steal into Tyler's heart. A moment later, though, he reflected on what Many Horse had just said.

You whites, as if she weren't one. Tyler wondered if he could ever forget who he was or where he came from. No sir, it'd be impossible. He came from Sweet Creek, Missouri, and would never shuck the name Bohannon like it was an old coat he'd outgrown.

That night when they settled themselves for sleep (Ooaya hardly ever objected anymore if he and Isaac talked), Tyler decided to break his vow not to speak to Isaac again about escaping. Having horses put a brand-new light on things. "You realize this changes everything, don't you, Isaac?" he asked.

"What does?"

"Horses. They can take us twice as far twice as fast. The snow's all gone now: we won't be easy to track. These folks are so taken up with plans to meet their relatives, they won't watch us so close for a while. We'll have a chance to—"

"But I want to see what's goin' on at the big get-together Iron Shell's headin' for," Isaac objected. "One Horn says some famous folks will be there."

"Famous folks?" Tyler scoffed. Isaac could think of more excuses not to talk about leaving than Sooner had fleas. "Indians don't have no famous folks that I ever heard about. Nobody like General Jo Shelby, not to mention Mr. Lincoln."

"Shows how much you know," Isaac said with a sniff.

"Name me some, then," Tyler challenged.

"One Horn says a fella named Red Cloud will be there. And another one named Crazy Horse. Once in the Moon of Trees Cracking—we call it December—Crazy Horse tricked eighty soldiers into a fight and killed 'em all."

"I don't hold with killing soldiers," Tyler retorted. The words weren't out of his mouth before he realized it was exactly what Black Jack Bohannon did. Papa had been in the business of killing Union soldiers. How much different could it be if a man named Crazy Horse did the same thing?

On the opposite side of the tipi, Tyler heard C'aske and Hepa cry out in their sleep. A moment later, Ooaya crooned to them in a tender mother's voice, and the boys were silent. Sometimes Mama had spoken in the same soft way to Rosa Lee, even to him and Lucas if they were sick or hurt.

Tyler frowned in the dark. It was simpler to believe the Sioux lived lives he'd never understand. He didn't want to think they had heroes or mothers who soothed children's nightmares. He was glad when Isaac started to snore. He didn't want to hear another word about Red Cloud or Crazy Horse.

The excitement that spread among the travelers ten days later was thick enough to taste. Even the horses quickened their pace, while some members of Iron Shell's band stopped to open their rawhide garment boxes and put on fancy beaded shirts or dresses, headdresses of hawk and eagle feathers, mocassins with porcupine quills dyed in the sacred Sioux colors of yellow, black, red, and white, and jewelry made of bone and turtle shell.

Many Horses stopped, too. When Tyler caught sight of her in her white doeskin dress, her oiled braids hanging straight down her back, his heart skipped a beat. She was so *pretty!* Prettier even than SallyJo McCarthy. Getting dressed up must mean the meeting place was near, Tyler realized, and toward late afternoon as the shadows in the grass grew long and soft, Ooaya reined her pony in on a ridge that overlooked a shallow valley.

Below, from one end of the valley to the other and all the way across, tipis glowed like pale cones in the failing light. Cook fires twinkled throughout the encampment. Dogs barked. Children's voices lifted high and clear on the dusky air. The smell of roasting meat rose to make Tyler's mouth water.

"Now ain't that a sight!" Isaac breathed. "Talk about a gatherin'! I kin see why these folks hustled to get here."

Ooaya picked a campsite, and Tyler began the familiar task of helping her unload the tipi poles, setting them up properly, then putting the smaller poles in place before draping sewn-together buffalo hides on the outside. The door faced east, as always. One by one, Ooaya's other possessions—skins for beds and the floor, Iron Shell's backrest, all of the rawhide bags, pouches, and boxes—were carried inside and set in place under her watchful eye.

The task was hardly finished when Tyler heard merry Sioux voices outside. Tyler peeked out and saw Ooaya welcome several women—her sisters or cousins, he guessed—and the women chattered like any gaggle of women who might gather in any town or village. A second later, though, Tyler saw something that made him groan with dismay.

During the move, the horses had been tethered close to the tipi each night to make it easy to get a fast start in the morning. Now, Iron Shell was taking his and Isaac's horses, Ooaya's pony, and Mouse back to the pony herd.

Tyler realized it meant he'd have to ask for help from Many Horses. He'd explain how Iron Shell planned to trade him off; how the whites would probably pack him off to Missouri; how he couldn't go home till he got his money and Elway's rifle back and settled a debt with Captain Little.

After her mother had paraded Many Horses all around the camp and she'd changed back into ordinary clothes, Tyler saw her helping Brown Shawl Woman get ready to cook the evening meal. He beckoned her to step aside for a moment. It was hard to know exactly where to begin, so he dived right in. Swiftly, he told her all about Captain Little, the theft of the money and the rifle, then about his biggest worry.

"Iron Shell will trade me off, on account of I'm not a treasure, like Isaac. He'll hang on to Isaac, but he'll get rid of me in a heartbeat. And those white folks that want to meet with the Seven Council Fires will probably send me back to Missouri."

Many Horses listened without speaking. Her glance was knowing. "And what you need is a horse so you can get away."

"Yes," Tyler answered. There was no sense beating around the bush. "Except there's no way I can get near the pony herd. If I tried to, it'd get me in big trouble. Killed, maybe."

"So you want me to help you."

"Yes, I do. Without you, there's no way I can make a run for it. You could pretend to go out to the herd to check on your mare and her new colt. Nobody would suspect anything."

"I cannot offend Iron Shell," Many Horses said firmly. "He's been kind to Brown Shawl Woman and me. I will think about it and give you my answer tomorrow."

Tyler decided to be as straight-up with Isaac as he'd been with Many Horses. In the morning while Ooaya fussed with the morning meal, he whispered, "Listen, Isaac, I think Many Horses will help us." He brushed quickly over the word *us*, as if he took it for granted Isaac would change his mind at the last minute.

"Help us do what?"

"She'll go out to the pony herd as if she wants to check on her mare and colt. If she can catch those two horses we been riding these past two weeks, we can strike out on our own."

Tyler wasn't surprised that Isaac retreated into silence. He was determined not to let it bother him. "There's one other thing," he said. Isaac hunched his shoulders up around his ears as if to shut out anything else Tyler had to say.

"When we leave, we'll take Many Horses with us."

Isaac stared at him in disbelief. "How come you thinks she wants to go?" he demanded. "Seems to me she likes bein' Brown Shawl Woman's daughter."

"It don't matter if she wants to or not," Tyler declared. "She should go back to her own folks. After we get up to Fort Benton and lay hands on Captain Little, we can figure out a way to get her back to Wichita, where she belongs."

Isaac drew a design on the ground with a stick, then rubbed it out with the toe of his mocassin. When he raised his glance again, Tyler saw an expression something like pity in his eyes.

"What's this 'us' and 'we' business, Ty? Don't you know you can't make people want what they don't want?" Isaac said. "If Many Horses don't want to go, how you aim to change her mind—or mine?"

"You're going to help me convince her," Tyler announced.

"I ain't goin' to do no such thing." There was something so unfamiliar in Isaac's voice that Tyler was momentarily wordless.

"You telling me that it ain't right for Many Horses to go back to Kansas?" he finally asked. "You telling me she shouldn't take up life as Mary Burden again? The only reason she's been here this long is because nobody gave her the courage to go home."

"What I'm tellin' you, Ty Bohannon, is you can't decide for her or for anybody else. Me included," Isaac said. His words were flinty. "Darned if I'll be a *ohoka* an' tell Many Horses what's right for her. Let her decide for herself."

"*Ohoka?*" Tyler echoed, grinding his teeth together. "What's that mean?"

Without waiting for a bowl of breakfast soup, Isaac turned on his heel and headed toward where One Horn and his cronies had gathered. "Means a hypocrite," he called over his shoulder, "an' I ain't goin' to be one. Not for you, not for nobody."

Tyler stared after him. Isaac's not the same person he was when we left Missouri, he realized. Isaac's head was high. His back was straight. It was plain that he wasn't one whit ashamed about being black. Out here on the Dakota prairie, he liked who he was. Iron Shell, Ooaya, the twins, One Horn—everyone in camp—liked him just the way he was. Now Isaac liked himself.

Folks back home claimed black people got uppity if you didn't keep them in their place. Was that what had happened to Isaac—he'd gotten all full of himself and too big for his britches? Or had he become the person the good Lord had always meant him to be?

Chapter Fourteen

No moon lighted the night sky, but it was filled with stars as hard and bright as bits of broken glass. Their gleam cast a faint silver sheen across the prairie as Tyler and Isaac crept out of Iron Shell's tipi.

They carried a few possessions with them—sleeping gear, a piece of flint for firemaking, Tyler's pocketknife, the rabbit stick One Horn had made for Isaac, scraps of food they'd managed to hoard. Outside, Tyler knelt to clamp his fingers around Sooner's muzzle.

"Don't let me hear a peep out of you, mister!" he whispered fiercely in the dog's ear. Nothing must go wrong now that Isaac had agreed to make a run for it. Only by reminding him of his own words had Tyler finally been able to convince him to do it.

"Remember how we started out back in Missouri?" Tyler asked on the second day at the new camp. Isaac gave him a wary look.

"As we headed down to St. Joe that morning, you said it was going to be me for you, and you for me, and I went along with you. You believed it then, same as me. We got to keep that kind of faith with each other, Isaac. It's how we started out. It's how we ought to finish."

For a long time Isaac didn't say a word. Then he nodded slowly, as if the words made sense. "Reckon you're right, Ty. If master had done right by my mama and daddy, things might not have turned out so bad for either one of 'em, or for me. So I won't go back on what I said. But maybe someday . . ." Isaac had let his words trail off, but Tyler understood what was in his heart: *Someday, maybe I'll come back to the People.*

Many Horses, who said she would explain later about not offending Iron Shell, was waiting for them not far from Brown Shawl Woman's tipi. No one spoke as they hurried across the shallow valley toward the pony herd, a large, dark blur at the narrowest end of the encampment.

When they got close to the herd, Many Horses warned in a low voice, "If Isaac's horse and the one you call Mouse aren't easy to find, you boys will have to take the first ones I can catch."

Tyler touched her shoulder lightly. "Be sure to get one for yourself, too," he said.

Many Horses turned, her dark eyes shiny and surprised in the starlight. "But I don't need—"

"Because you're going to come with us," Tyler said. Although Isaac had agreed to leave Iron Shell's camp, he still stoutly refused to encourage Many Horses to do the same. Tyler knew he'd have to persuade her himself.

"There are things you know about the prairie that it'll take me and Isaac half a lifetime to learn," he explained. "If we hope to make a clean getaway, we're going to need plenty of help from someone like you. So you got to come with us, at least for a while."

Once they were far from camp, when Many Horses didn't feel the powerful tug of loyalty to Brown Shawl Woman, it would be easier to remind her that she was white. That her name was really Mary Burden, that once she'd lived in Wichita. When it was only the three of them together, Tyler was sure he could convince her to go clear on to Fort Benton.

Many Horses gave him a long, careful look. She simply nodded, as if she understood what Tyler had left unsaid.

Because the encampment in the valley was so large, with many warriors available to fend off the *hohes,* Iron Shell had posted only four sentries around his herd. Many Horses went forward, making a soft, clicking noise with her tongue against her teeth. A moment later Tyler saw the white-footed mare come forward in the starlight, followed by her gangly colt. Many Horses held out her hand, and Tyler realized she had a piece of prairie turnip in it. The mare took it eagerly, then Many Horses slipped a leather bit into the mare's mouth and fitted the bridle over her ears.

She passed the reins to Tyler without a word, then

disappeared like a shadow into the rest of the herd. Many Horses's scent—pure Sioux and familiar to the animals—meant that none of the horses raised their heads in alarm. First, she caught Mouse, whose pale gray color reflected the faint starlight, making him easy to find. Next, she caught Isaac's long-legged, speckled horse.

Many Horses beckoned Isaac and Tyler to follow her away from the herd, into the shelter of a narrow ravine, out of sight of those guarding the horses.

The threesome mounted silently. Many Horses, who'd had much more practice, did so in a single, fluid movement. Isaac heaved himself three times at the side of his tall horse before he was able to throw a leg over its back. Tyler led Mouse to the side of the ravine, moved to its highest side, grabbed a hunk of the pony's mane, and mounted on the second try.

Rather than ride away from camp bold and upright, Many Horses leaned low over her mare's neck so she wouldn't present a silouette against the skyline. Tyler and Isaac followed her example. Sooner, who seemed to understand the gravity of the moment, crept along soundlessly, head lowered and belly flat to the ground.

When they reached the ridge above the camp, Many Horses halted her mare. Below, hundreds and hundreds of tipis belonging to the Seven Council Fires glowed like pewter ornaments in the starlight. The creek running through the camp twisted casually this way and that like a silver ribbon dropped by a girl who'd forgotten to pick it up.

In his own unwilling bones, the sight below exerted the same powerful claim on Tyler as on the hearts and heads of Isaac and Many Horses. If they lingered here too long, he knew one or both of them might be tempted to change their minds.

"We'd better hurry," he whispered. "It must be past midnight. We need to put as many miles between us and this place as we can before the sun comes up and everyone figures out what happened."

In the silvery light, Tyler couldn't make out the expressions on the dark faces of either Many Horses or Isaac, but when he urged Mouse forward, they both followed silently. His first impulse was to put Mouse into a full gallop, but Many Horses cautioned him against such foolishness.

"The hooves of running horses cause vibrations in the earth that can be felt by anyone sleeping on the ground. Early in life, the People are trained to be alert to such things. Someone—it could be a child as young as C'aske or Hepa—might call out an alarm. It is best to move slowly for many more miles."

At last the night sky paled. Only then did Many Horses finally put her mare into an easy gallop. They rode without halting until the earth turned toward the sun and the light of the stars was extinguished.

Tyler estimated they must have covered several miles—fifteen, maybe—before the sun finally slid over the edge of the world. As it did, Many Horses stopped, faced the east with her arms spread wide as if to embrace the orange ball on the horizon. She began to chant:

> "Welcome, welcome, Great presence,
> You, who make the whole earth bright
> And bring new grass for the buffalo.
> Bless the Seven Council Fires,
> Bring luck to my friends, Tyler and Isaac,
> And keep the prairie safe for the People."

Then she pointed to a shallow stream that threaded its way through the grass. "We will travel in water now," she said. "On the prairie our tracks will be easy to follow, but water will leave no trace that we've passed this way."

Single file, with Sooner bringing up the rear, they entered the creek and followed it northwest for many miles. When it was past midday, Isaac finally called out, "Folks, I am purely starved to death! Ain't it time for us to stop awhile and eat?"

Tyler smiled. Isaac and his belly!

They dismounted and let the horses graze by the edge of the creek while Tyler and Isaac unpacked the scraps of food they'd hoarded for more than a week. Many Horses, who hadn't known she'd be taking such a long journey, had brought nothing to eat. When Tyler offered her part of his share, she gave him a rueful smile.

"I agreed to come with you," she said, "but I did not agree to stay with you. Save your food for yourselves, because when this day ends, I will return to camp."

"But you can't!" Tyler yelled. The camp was miles away now, so he wasn't afraid to raise his voice. "Without your help, Iron Shell will catch us for sure!"

Many Horses shook her head. "You wanted horses, and I got you horses. You wanted to be pointed in the right direction, and I pointed you in the right direction," she reminded him. "But I'm not going with you to that place you talked about, to Fort Benton." Then she gave Tyler a sly, wise grin. "And not to Wichita, either. Now eat quickly, so we can move on."

"You have to!" Tyler squawked after he and Isaac had gobbled a few bites and they'd all remounted. Many Horses put her mare into the creek again, and they traveled along single file. Tyler hadn't planned to start lecturing her so soon, but she'd forced his hand. "You have to, because your name ain't really Many Horses," he reminded her. "It's Mary Burden!"

"In a while, this creek will enter a larger one," Many Horses said, paying no attention to his noisy argument, "and after that into a larger one. I will wait until you have crossed safely to the other side—but I won't cross with you."

"Sure you will!" Tyler insisted, the horses' splashing feet punctuating his words. "You're *white,* don't you understand? Come with us, we'll get you back to where you belong!" When Many Horses still wasn't moved a whit, Tyler tried the same thing with her that had worked with Isaac. He threw her own words back at her.

"You told me one day about what happened to the Cherokees, how they lost everything and ended up dying on a long journey you said was called the Trail of Tears. You're the one who told me how settlers have killed off so many buffalo that Iron Shell has to hunt longer and harder and sometimes folks in camp go hungry. That fate doesn't have to be yours!"

Many Horses halted, turned to face Tyler, and folded her palms across the neck of her mare. She studied her knuckles, then looked straight at him. "Long ago, I tried to save my little brother, whose name I think was Willy, though I can't remember for sure. When I try to bring my mother's face to mind, her features are only a shadow." She paused, then went on with sigh.

"Because of such things, my heart doesn't feel white anymore. When Brown Shawl Woman spoke for me, she might have saved my life. She honored me by calling me Many Horses, the name of the daughter she'd loved and lost long before I ever came to the People. She treated me as if I were her own child. She taught me how to tan buffalo hides, how to make a deer's skin as soft as a baby's, and how to make *wasna*."

"But you'll never have another chance like this one!" Tyler objected, his voice hot with conviction. "Sooner or later, Iron Shell will have to sign a treaty. He'll have to promise to keep his people on that place they're going to call a reservation. Besides, he'll be madder'n hops at you for helping us. What'll happen to you when he finds out?"

"I cannot say," Many Horses admitted. "I will explain to him that you and Isaac came from my old tribe, that I helped you in their name, not in my own." She set her lips firmly. "It would break Brown Shawl Woman's heart if I ran away—therefore, I will not betray her."

Betrayal was all Tyler had thought about since Captain Little had served him and Isaac up to Iron Shell like two boiled potatoes on a plate. The way Many Horses used the word now made him realize he couldn't argue with her anymore. He didn't even want to. Many Horses had decided not to betray the confidence of the woman who'd saved her life. It was a decision that—almost against his will—Tyler admired beyond words.

They traveled in silence the rest of the afternoon. Then, as Many Horses predicted, the creek widened and emptied into a larger one. "We call it Place Where Deer Come to Drink," she said. "Once, our hunters lay in ambush here and killed many. Soon, this stream will empty into another, then finally into the one you call the Missouri. Follow it, and you will reach your destination."

Many Horses urged her mare out of the water and

halfway up the east side of the creek bank. The colt followed nimbly behind, and began to nurse greedily at his mother's belly.

The time to part had come too soon, too soon. Tyler's heart felt bruised and tender as he realized he'd likely never see this girl again. Long ago, he'd stood on a different riverbank and said good-bye to Papa. He'd never looked on him again, either.

"Are you sure—" Tyler began wistfully. This time he didn't yell. His voice was merely hopeful. But before he could go on, Many Horses held up her hand to silence any final pleas.

"It is not meant that I go with you," she murmured. Tyler noticed that the smile she gave him held no regret. No tears glimmered in her eyes; no tremor made her voice quiver. "My heart isn't white anymore," she had said, and meant it.

"You must hurry. I will wait here till you have crossed to the other side. You can still cover a few more miles before you make camp tonight." Then, before he could do as she said, Many Horses judged her mare closer to Mouse. She held out her hand.

"Open your palm," she said. Tyler did, and in it she laid a smooth stone, speckled lightly with brown, about the size of a prairie chicken's egg. Her dark eyes held his blue ones for only a moment.

"*Wapatanyan,*" she whispered softly. "Be lucky."

Tyler and Isaac, their horses up to their knees in

water, proceeded toward the fork where the creek emptied into the river. They went upstream a hundred yards till they found a likely crossing place. The river at that point was no more than two or three feet deep, not enough to force the horses to swim.

On the other side, Tyler turned to wave farewell to Many Horses, the stone already as warm as a beating heart in his hand. He'd never think of her as Mary Burden again. Of her own free will she'd chosen to be one of the People, a member of the Seven Council Fires. She'd always be Many Horses now.

But the bare knoll, its pale spring grass waving lightly in the wind, was deserted. A moment later, to the east, where the sky was already somber and broody with coming night, Tyler caught a final glimpse of her.

She had urged her mare into a gallop. The long-legged colt ran swiftly at its mother's side, while Many Horses's thick brown braids trailed behind her on the wind. She turned once to wave, her face obscured in shadow, one hand lifted high against the sky. She spread her five fingers in the air, then was swallowed up by the vast prairie.

Tyler felt a suspicious burning sensation behind his eyes. His throat was dry. He was grateful that Isaac didn't offer a single word of sympathy.

As they turned to the west where rosy light still lingered, Tyler remembered a day long ago at Sweet Creek when he'd had a terrible fight with Lucas. Afterward, they'd lain side by side staring up at the sky, a pair of battered and regretful brothers, while overhead the piercing cry of a redtail hawk sounded like something breaking.

Far from home, on the stark prairie of Dakota Territory, Tyler Bohannon felt his heart break again.

CHAPTER FIFTEEN

Living under Ooaya's thumb day and night, never free to traipse off like Isaac did had made Tyler feel mean and sad. He had longed to be free. Now he was.

What he never counted on was how hard it would be to find food and shelter to go along with freedom. Once or twice he even thought about the stern comforts of Iron Shell's tipi with something like affection.

The first night after he and Isaac parted from Many Horses, they built a small fire in a grove of willows next to the river. They ate, banked the fire with some green wood, then crawled under the lip of an overhanging bank close to the water. The protected spot kept the wind, which turned cold the minute the sun went down, from sneaking down their collars or sticking its fingers through the rips of their buckskin shirts.

The scraps of food they had hoarded lasted two

days. The third day, Isaac began to use his rabbit stick, but missed oftener than he connected with his prey. The first rabbit he killed was swiftly skinned, cooked till it was barely warmed through, then eaten almost raw. While the boys feasted, Sooner dined on the entrails.

"Many Horses did the right thing," Isaac mused, licking red juice off his fingers. "I sure wouldn't want to put a female person through this kind a misery—not even one that's lived a long time with Indians. Brown Shawl Woman will take better care of her than we could."

"When I asked her to come with us, I never promised it would be easy," Tyler snapped. Isaac had no danged business reminding him of Many Horses. Even without Isaac's reminder, though, Tyler thought about her every night as he drifted off to sleep. The memory of her caused the same kind of ache under his ribs that he got every time he thought of Papa.

Was he too young to love a girl the way grown-ups loved each other? The way Mama and Papa must have loved each other once upon a time? Deep inside, that's sure what it felt like. Many Horses had talked about marrying someone from the Seven Council Fire, but Tyler imagined taking her back to Sweet Creek . . . he would tell Mama and Elway—Oat Snepp, too—"I want you to meet my friend, Mary Burden." He might even mention they would be married someday. It was a foolish dream, because she wasn't Mary Burden anymore.

• • •

Seven days later, when he and Isaac spied a sod shanty silhouetted against the sky some distance from the river, the prospect of real food cooked by a homesteader's wife—biscuits, gravy, meat that for a change wasn't raw—made Tyler's mouth water. As they got closer, however, it was plain the place had been abandoned.

Weeds grew thickly beside the path leading up to the shack. On the front side a makeshift door hung slant-wise on its hinges. Tyler pulled it ajar and peered into the single square dark room. It was more like the cave of an animal than a place where people had lived. He was about to close the door when he noticed a square of yellowed paper tacked on the inside. He read aloud what it said.

"'It were too Hard. My woman died.
The children got sick.
160 Acres ain't worth Brakin a man's Heart.'"

Isaac listened and stared off across the landscape that was as flat as a table top. "A hun'ert and sixty acres in country like this don't amount to much, Ty. Where I come from, folks said the ground was so rich, you could stick nails in it and they'd grow." He sighed. "Why do you reckon Iron Shell and his kin travel from one end of this land t'other? 'Cause there ain't no place that invites settlin' down permanent, that's why."

The occupants of the sod house had left behind a

half-full tin of corn meal, a few spoons of rancid bacon drippings in a chipped blue cup, and some dried beans in a sack riddled with holes chewed by mice.

While Isaac staked the horses, Tyler picked weevils out of the cornmeal, then stirred the bacon drippings and some river water together to make a pitiful excuse for griddle cakes. Using a flat stone, he cooked them over a fire that Isaac built of trash he found inside the shack. They ate silently, giving Sooner his share, and spent the night on the floor of the abandoned building. When they moved on in the morning, Tyler took along the chipped cup, the can of cornmeal, and the beans.

One afternoon they found some fish trapped in a shallow backwater pool along the edge of the river. "They's six of 'em here!" Isaac cried joyously. He scooped them out with his bare hands and threw them up on the bank. They were medium-sized speckled trout with rosy stripes down their sides. Isaac gutted them while Tyler cut willow spears to roast them over a fire. Even without salt, Tyler was sure he'd never tasted anything better, and Sooner feasted on the heads and tails.

Ooaya had taught Tyler how to dig prairie turnips and onions, which was an important part of doing women's work. He used the empty cornmeal can as a pot. With water, a few beans, turnips and onions, and leaves from a sage bush he concocted a thin soup that only made him and Isaac hungrier.

Isaac rigged up a snare out of strips Tyler tore off his threadbare blanket and sometimes caught a prairie chicken. No matter what they tried, though, there was never enough to eat. Sooner's sides caved in, creating dark hollows along his red shanks. Out of desperation he took to eating beetles and grasshoppers.

"Reckon we'll end up doin' likewise," Isaac said. Tyler inspected his own ribs. He'd done the same thing when he went to Texas to find Papa. Now they stuck out so far that he was sure he could've played a tune on them—maybe one of Captain Little's cheery little ballads. No padding was left on his rump, so he often slid off Mouse's back and walked beside him because riding was too miserable.

Mouse and Buddy—Isaac had named his spotted horse the day they watched Many Horses ride away—were luckier. They ate their fill of rich prairie grass every night, until their coats gleamed and their bellies were round.

Tyler found a stick and notched it with his thumbnail to count off the days, just as Many Horses had done after her rescue from the Crows. He'd carefully marked off five whole weeks' worth of days when the stick disappeared.

"You seen that little stick I been using to keep track of the days?" Tyler asked Isaac.

"It don't matter if you count 'em or not," Isaac said as Tyler searched for it. "We'll get where we're goin' when we get there. Keepin' track of the days ain't goin' to make it happen a minute quicker."

Tyler frowned. Had Isaac taken the stick and burned it on purpose? He was about to give him a bawling out, then realized it was stupid to suspect such a thing. This was no time to turn on each other.

As the hot prairie days and cold prairie nights drifted by, Tyler and Isaac spoke to each other only when it was necessary. Talking took way too much energy. Hunger dominated their every thought.

They followed Sooner's example and began to eat beetles and grasshoppers. Roasted, they weren't too bad, except for the crunchy sound they made as a person chewed. They ate the eggs of meadowlarks raw. They roasted a turtle they found near the river (Tyler had to shut his eyes and ears when Isaac crushed its shell with a rock). Once, they surprised three young snakes warming themselves on a rock, beheaded them, and roasted them whole.

Through it all, only one thing kept Tyler going. Eventually, he knew he was bound to catch up with Captain Little.

Many Horses explained that she'd never been to Fort Benton herself. Only raiding parties went there, she said, because that was Blackfeet country, who were as heartily despised by the Sioux as the Crows. Yet she'd heard stories about what the country looked like and knew of a landmark to be watched for.

"When you come to the Place of White Walls, you will know you are close to your destination," she told Tyler. But on the day that tall, chalky cliffs finally loomed like white walls on either side of the Missouri, Tyler was too hungry and too tired to be thrilled by the sight.

A few days later, he and Isaac reined Mouse and Buddy to a halt on the east side of an overlook above Fort Benton in Montana Territory. It had rained in the afternoon, and the air was fragrant. In the mild gloom of the summer evening the light of a few gas lamps along the town's boardwalk was reflected in the muddy main street below. The Missouri could be seen winding through the town, and a half dozen steamboats were tied at the levee.

"I sure don't see no keelboat down there," Isaac whispered, his voice raspy with fatigue. "We mighta come all this way for nothin'."

"It's too dim to see for sure," Tyler muttered. "We'll look for Captain Little in the morning. What we need to do now is get us a place to stay."

He'd been willing to sleep in a livery stable in St. Joe, but that was a whole lifetime ago. Now Tyler craved the feel of a real bed under his bones, warm water to wash his face, real food to eat. Of course, a place to stay brought up the subject of money. When they'd left St.

Joe they'd both had some. Now, Isaac was the only one who did.

"You willing to use some of your money so we can get ourselves a bed tonight? You won't be out anything because I'll make my half up soon's I lay hands on Captain Little and get back what's due me."

"*If* you lay hands on Cap'n Little," Isaac corrected. "It's not for sure he came all this way. He lied about so much, he'd lie about coming here, too. I'd just as soon never lay eyes on that old fool again."

But the captain's cheery face with its twinkly eyes, rosy cheeks, and white beard had never been far from Tyler's thoughts, even in the darkest days in Iron Shell's camp.

Revenge . . . that's what he wanted. The word itself, let alone the deed, was as tart and sweet as lemon and sugar when Tyler rolled it on his tongue. Now, so close to getting it, he realized there was something else he wanted maybe even more.

He wanted to know *why*. Why had the old man betrayed him and Isaac? Why had he sold them into a life that could've meant death for both of them?

Tyler couldn't explain it, even to himself, but Captain Little's betrayal was all mixed up in his head with Black Jack Bohannon's decision not to come home to Sweet Creek. If an answer could be wrung out of the captain, then what Papa did might make more sense. Because for the first time in his life, Tyler realized he hated Papa a little. Hated him for doing what the captain had done. Hated him for being a betrayer.

Mouse and Buddy sensed the end of the journey was near, and quickened their steps as Tyler and Isaac rode down a rutted wagon road into Fort Benton. The blockhouse of the fort could be seen at the far end of the town, whose inhabitants were so accustomed to seeing newcomers of all shapes and sizes disembark from the steamers that they paid Tyler and Isaac no special mind.

Isaac's memory was long, however. "You think folks out here are goin' to be upset about me bein' black?" he wondered aloud.

"Bet they don't know much about black folks here, Isaac. Anyway, it'll be like it's always been: We're traveling together, so if somebody takes me in, they got to take you, too."

The sign in front of a small, square, unpainted house at the edge of town announced, MRS. FITCH'S. BEDS. BOARD. REASONABLE.

"Wonder what she calls 'reasonable,'" Tyler said, licking his chapped lips. "If we aim to get on out there to California, we can't throw our money around. I reckon we could pay twenty-five cents a night, but not a penny more." He moistened his lips again.

"I don't relish the idea of cheating anyone, Isaac. Just the same, I'm goin' to rent a room as if it's only me that's going to use it. Then we'll figure out a way to sneak you in, which will cut our expenses right in half."

After Isaac fished some money from his pocket, Tyler motioned him to go up the street, then he tied Mouse to the rack in front of the boardinghouse. A big woman who looked a lot like Cousin Clayton's mama—stout, with lots of solid meat on her bones—opened the door.

"I'm l-l-looking to r-r-rent me a room for a night or two," Tyler stammered. He hated the notion of pulling a fast one on a lady who looked so much like Aunt Margaret. "I got money to pay," he added quickly, to take the edge off his guilt.

"Why, you're a whole lot younger than most fellers that stop here," the woman said. She smiled, which made her look friendlier than Aunt Margaret. "But what about your friend? When I looked out a minute ago I swear I saw another lad with you, one on a spotted horse. He have folks hereabouts that he aims to stay with?"

Tyler studied his feet. "No, ma'am, he don't." He sighed and looked her straight in the eye. "Truth is, I was fixing to cheat you. We're short of money, Isaac and me, so I was going to rent a room, then sneak him in when you wasn't looking, so two of us could stay for the price of one."

"Cheat me, were you!" the woman exclaimed. She braced her fists on her hips and studied him closely. Aunt Margaret would've smacked him alongside the head for such impertinence, so he braced himself for a blow.

"Well, you look as if you could stand a wash and a

good meal," she said kindly. "Your friend, too, I wager. As it happens, I got space for you tonight, and—if you can afford it—I'll let the pair of you stay for forty cents, which is a bargain at twenty cents apiece."

Tyler bowed slightly. "That'd suit us fine, ma'am." He raked his hand through his hair. "There's one other thing. Can my dog sleep on your porch? He's a good dog and won't cause you no grief."

"It'll be fine, providing he don't make a fuss. After all, I know what it's like to have a pet." She pointed to a white cat sitting on the windowsill. "Amanda's the best company a widow woman could ask for."

Tyler cleared his throat. "Um . . . there's something else I oughta mention. My friend—well, Isaac's skin ain't the same color as mine. Is that going to make a difference?"

The woman drew her brows together and frowned. "He's Indian, you mean? Folks around here aren't real partial to Indians, especially after what happened out there at the Winslow place two weeks ago. Some Blackfeet scoundrels ran off their beef cattle, stole three horses, and burned down the barn. My other boarders would take offense, son."

"No, ma'am," Tyler replied. "My friend ain't red. He's—ah—Isaac's black."

"Black!" Mrs. Fitch's eyes grew round with surprise. "He's one a them freed persons I heard about?"

"The same," Tyler assured her. "Beholden to no one

but himself now that the war between the blue and gray is over."

"My sympathies were of an abolitionist persuasion," Mrs. Fitch confided, "so it's no matter to me. Bring him along—if you can afford forty cents, that is. Which will include chicken and biscuits for supper and oatmeal mush in the morning, not to mention there's a shed out back for your horses."

Chicken and biscuits! Oatmeal mush!

Tyler was sure he'd never heard more wonderful words. "Oh yes, ma'am. We can afford it," he assured her. He whistled to Isaac. Sooner arrived first, with Isaac close behind.

Tyler made Sooner understand that he'd have to stay quietly on the porch, then he and Isaac stepped inside Mrs. Fitch's boardinghouse. It was small and tidy, and from the back of the house came the unmistakable smell of frying chicken. Mrs. Fitch directed him and Isaac up a flight of narrow stairs.

"Farthest room down the hall, on the left," she said. "I'll bring up warm water soon's I turn that chicken. Unless my nose tells me wrong, you boys could use some soap, too."

Tyler and Isaac walked carefully up the stairs and tiptoed down the hall. The room was tiny, hardly bigger than a pantry. A faded green curtain hung at the window, and a large basin and pitcher of cold water stood on a washstand. Tyler sat on the edge of the bed and didn't say a word. He hadn't been in a house with walls or smelled chicken frying for almost a year. He'd been so busy trying to stay alive, he hadn't realized how much he missed such pleasures. "It's real nice," he whispered.

"You ain't just whistlin' Dixie," Isaac agreed.

After Mrs. Fitch delivered the warm water—*warm water!*—they took turns washing. Tyler scrubbed his face, dug the dirt out of his ears, and even dabbed at his ripe armpits before they went downstairs. Four men sat at the table, and before anyone ate, the one with a grizzled beard said grace.

"Bless these vittles and us that eats 'em," he declared, then everyone dug in. Afterward, Tyler asked Mrs. Fitch for a few scraps, and carried them out to Sooner. An hour later, he and Isaac stretched out side by side in bed. Oh, the wonder of a mattress, even one that sagged in the middle! They fell asleep before they could say good night.

After eating mush with a sprinkle of sugar and a tablespoon of milk—Mrs. Fitch measured the milk herself, so no one at the table took more than his share—Tyler and Isaac left the boardinghouse and headed for the river on foot.

"If the captain's here, he'll stick tighter'n a tick to the *Darlin' Nell*," Tyler predicted.

"Not to mention what's aboard her," Isaac reminded him.

Although they hadn't been able to see a keelboat from the bluff above town, at the south end of the levee, their first stopping point, there was the *Darlin' Nell*. The red, gold-trimmed name on her bow looked as merry as ever, but no one was aboard. Tyler peered into the cargo box. It was empty.

"What you boys lookin' for?" inquired a voice behind them. Tyler and Isaac turned to face an official-looking man with a sheaf of papers in his hand. "I'm the wharf-master," he said. "Maybe I can help you."

"We're looking for the crew of the *Darlin' Nell*," Tyler said, which wasn't exactly the truth. The ship's captain was the only one who mattered.

"Well now, we had to stick those fellas in the lockup," the man said. "They cleaned out the old man who owned this tub. He put up an awful squawk, because they worked him over good. When they was finished with him, he wasn't a pretty sight."

If Captain Little were dead, how could Elway's Winchester or the money ever be retrieved? "Worked him over good?" Tyler whispered. "You mean they did him in?"

"No, no, son, he ain't dead. Might be close to, though. We don't have a hospital in these parts, so we put 'im in the infirmary that the Jesuits operate up there at the old fort." The man cocked his head and rustled his papers. "You kin to the old codger?" he asked curiously.

"Surely am," Tyler answered. Kin would probably be allowed to see someone in an infirmary more easily than a stranger. "He's my uncle on my mama's side of the family. Name's Richard Little."

"Yep, that's him all right," the wharfmaster agreed, pausing to give Isaac a quizzical glance. Like the Sioux, he might never have seen a black person before. "You go on up there to the fort and I bet the brothers will give you permission to see the old fellow."

"You mean the fort ain't a fort anymore?" Tyler asked.

"Hasn't been since a year before the Civil War. The Jesuits have a mission there now. Among other charities, they opened an infirmary for down-on-their-luck folks such as your uncle."

The brother who greeted Tyler and Isaac folded his hands over his brown robe and studied them regretfully. "I'd better warn you that the knocks and bruises your uncle got are only part of his worries," he said as if he hoped to soften the news he was about to deliver.

"Only part of his worries?" Tyler echoed.

"His heart's wore out," the monk said. "The terrible drubbing he took from his crew only hastened what was in store for him. When he leaves here, I suspect it'll be to make a short trip to the cemetery atop the bluff yonder." With a brown-sleeved arm he gestured to a site west of town, where a few grave markers were silhouetted against the blue morning sky.

The infirmary itself was a small, whitewashed room with six narrow cots in it and a single high window at the far end. Only three cots were occupied, two by thin young men who looked as if they were recovering from the flu like Papa got before the war.

The occupant of the third had turned his face to the wall, but his bulk and the tangle of dirty white hair spread across the pillow made it plain who it was. Together, Tyler and Isaac moved forward and stood at the side of the cot.

Captain Little stirred fretfully, as if rising out of a troubled dream. He seemed to sense someone at his side, and rolled over. Tyler drew in his breath.

This man bore no relation to St. Nicholas. The captain's cheeks weren't round and pink anymore. Illness had turned the puckery nests around his eyes into gray puddles. A deep gash sliced down the middle of his forehead. The bruise on his neck had started to turn green around the edges. His bulbous nose was more swollen than ever, and two of his snaggly, tobacco-stained front teeth were missing.

"Why, if it ain't those runaways, one of 'em pale, the other one dusky," the captain murmured with a trace of his old foxy slyness. "Never thought I'd look on you boys again." He seemed neither surprised nor embarrassed to see them.

"I'm here to settle up with you," Tyler said, pleased by the businesslike tone in his voice. It was worthy of Elway Snepp himself. "You got my money and you got my rifle, Captain Little. I'm here to get 'em back, and I don't intend to leave without 'em."

Chapter Sixteen

"Those rascals I called a crew took your money, laddie," Captain Little croaked. "They picked my pockets like they was pluckin' an old rooster." He wadded up his pillow and stuffed it under his head so he could comfortably eyeball Tyler and Isaac.

"Took everything else, too. The bangles and beads, every pot and pan, even them bright bolts of gingham," he added with a bitter laugh.

Tyler stepped closer to the cot and bent over the captain. "Did they take the contraband, too—all that ammunition and the rifles you had stashed in the cargo box?" he asked, knowing perfectly well they had.

"Contraband?" The word caught the captain off guard, and he blinked with surprise. Tyler noticed the sly merriment of bygone days had vanished from the old man's eyes.

"You know doggone well you weren't s'posed to trade rifles to the Indians," Tyler said before the captain could deny he'd done such a thing. "It's against the law. That's why you hid 'em way at the back of the cargo box, labeled 'em SCISSORS, NEEDLES, AND AWLS, and had a fit about anyone goin' in there."

Captain Little sighed. "They made off with it soon after we docked, son. Had it peddled before I realized what they were up to. When I objected—and I did, loud enough to be heard clear to the Land of the Grand-mother—the whole bunch beat me, all of 'em at once." He laid his hand across his chest as if to quiet the rat-tling of his heart as he recalled the thrashing he'd taken.

"They told me I was a wicked old man, not fit to live with decent folks," he muttered, a note of astonishment in his voice. "They claimed swappin' you and your darky chum off to Iron Shell made me a pariah. A pariah! Said I deserved to be cast out of the human race." That the crew had been as ruthless as he'd been himself seemed to puzzle the captain.

"I suppose they took my rifle, too," Tyler prodded, realizing it was too much to hope that it had been over-looked.

A faint gleam of his old craftiness suddenly lighted the captain's rheumy eyes. "No, sir, that's one thing they didn't get!" he exclaimed. "See, I toted it with me every-where I went. To keep it safe, you know, in case I ever ran into you again. Then I met a fella aboard one of the steamers who took a shine to it almost the minute we docked and offered to pay me twice what it was worth. I couldn't turn 'im down."

Captain Little gave Tyler a feeble smile. "I figgered it'd be a month of Sundays before you got away from Iron Shell, so I decided to pocket the money—to keep it safe for you in case we met again, of course—but it was among what those fellers took off me."

Elway's rifle was gone. The money was gone. It meant there really wasn't much left to talk about. It was of little comfort to know that Henry and Luther and the others stole the captain blind partly because they didn't approve of what he'd done back there at the cove.

The news was so disheartening that Tyler almost forgot there was something else he'd intended to wring out of the captain.

"*Why*, Captain Little?" he demanded, his voice unnaturally loud. The captain looked up at him, perturbed, and adjusted his pillow. "Why what, laddie?" he echoed dazedly.

"You gave your solemn promise you'd treat me and Isaac fair if we treated you fair. We did. But you went ahead and traded us off like we was no different than a handful of beads or a couple pots. What I want to know is *why*."

Tyler's question hung unanswered on the air. Dust motes shimmered in a shaft of sunlight that came through the high window at the end of the room. As the captain struggled with an answer, his battered face crumbled slowly, like a plaything made of mud that Rosa Lee had left out in the rain. It was hard to imagine that Richard Little's mustache had ever quivered comically like a cat's whiskers or that he'd ever looked like a kindly character in a Christmas story. He was just a tired old wreck of a man now.

"I ran out on my family a long time ago, laddie," Captain Little began softly, his voice cracking in the middle of each sentence. "I traded my wife for another woman—for my *Darlin' Nell*—and for a life of adventure on the river. My wife's gone now, rest her soul, but I never forgot my boys. My boys, my boys . . ." He lingered over the last four words with sad and tender affection.

"To make a long story short, laddie, I figgered if I could I'd make a couple more trips up the river and make good trades—and nothin' trades better in Indian country than rifles and ammunition—so I decided to break the law and do exactly that," he whispered. "When I had me a hatful of money, I aimed to go back and make it up to Mark and Paul and William."

Captain Little plucked at his bedclothes, his words momentarily bright with pictures of how it would be when his sons welcomed him home.

"Except that fool Bodie went and ruined everything," he said, his voice suddenly angry. "For a minute, it looked like Iron Shell would kill me. If that happened, my boys would never know I remembered 'em. If the chief slit my throat, which he plainly intended to do, it'd be all over. The only choice I had was to turn you boys over to him and hope he'd spare my life." There was no apology in Captain Little's voice, or any shame written on his face.

Tyler had almost forgotten that Isaac was standing right beside him until he spoke up. "Your boys didn't want a hatful of money, Cap'n," Isaac said. "They only wanted their daddy to come home."

The idea seemed to confuse the old man. "But I loved the river, don't you see?" he protested. "I never meant to be gone so long. . . ."

"You made a choice," Tyler pointed out coolly. "You betrayed your own sons, so it was easy to betray me and Isaac, even though we always did right by you."

Papa had made a choice, too, hadn't he? He'd wanted to start the war all over again with a misguided notion of recovering honor for the South. Robert E. Lee had surrendered nobly—had admitted the long ordeal was over—but not Papa. No sir, not Black Jack Bohannon. In his way, he was as misguided as Captain Little.

Tyler stared down at the figure on the cot. The captain looked oddly small and harmless, his formerly pink cheeks grayer than day-old porridge. The monk said the beating he'd taken was the least of his worries. Did Richard Little know he was headed for the cemetery on the hill, that his sons would never know he'd wanted to come home?

In spite of himself, Tyler felt a twinge of pity for the old man. It was mingled with pity for Papa, too. He touched Papa's letter that still rested against his heart. Neither man had understood until too late what he'd turned his back on.

"We got to go now, Cap'n," Tyler announced, surprised by the lightness of spirit that he felt. He'd come here this morning planning to berate and harangue the old man, to beat on him with words like the crew of the *Darlin' Nell* beat him with fists. None of that mattered anymore.

"I never meant to do you harm," the captain whispered. "You were savvy boys. I figgered somehow you'd be all right."

"Good-bye, Captain," Tyler said, turning on his heel. The desire for revenge, which had been so sweet and had kept him going so long, was gone. As with so many things, Isaac had been right: If he hung on to it he'd betray himself, just like Papa and the captain had betrayed themselves.

"I just wanted to go home with a hatful of"—Captain Little called after him—"a hatful of money for Mark and Paul and William to make up for bein' gone so long. . . ."

Tyler and Isaac strode past the two pale young men who dozed lightly on their cots, out of the infirmary, past three brown-robed brothers in the courtyard who were cutting wood, then out of the mission itself. For the first time in longer than he could say, Tyler's head felt clear. His business in Fort Benton was done.

"We'll take us another day's rest here," he told Isaac as they headed back to Mrs. Fitch's. "Then we'll move on. For a while I'll be in your debt, on account of I still don't have any money. But I'll figure out a way to earn some as we—"

Before he could outline the rest of his plan, Isaac stopped dead in his tracks and pointed. "Looka there, Ty," he breathed. "Don't that one look prettier'n a peeled onion? Clean as a whistle and as shiny as if she'd been painted this morning. . . ."

Those words turned the clock back nearly a year, to the evening on the levee at St. Joe. Tyler turned to stare in the direction Isaac was pointing. The name on the bow of the sleek sternwheeler was *Undaunted.* When Tyler glanced up at the wheelhouse, he saw the same scowling captain who'd had no use for runaways or a dog with the eyes of a born killer.

In the bright light of the summer morning in Montana Territory, however, the captain of the *Undaunted* didn't look as sour as Tyler remembered. He turned and beckoned with a smile to someone behind him in the wheelhouse. Tyler took a step backward and steadied himself against Isaac when he saw who came to lean against the rail beside the captain.

"Greatgodamighty!" he whispered, barely able to get the words out.

Standing beside the captain of the *Undaunted,* as comfortable as if they'd been running the river their whole lives, were Elway Snepp and Lucas Bohannon.

The gleaming, blue-barreled Winchester rested comfortably in the crook of Elway's arm, and Lucas's grin was as wide as a mile.

"C'mon up, boys," the captain called genially.

Lucas was an inch taller than when Tyler saw him last, and now looked him square in the eye. There was a cocky assurance about him that made him a very different boy from the glum one who'd waited beside Elway's wagon while Elway and Rosa Lee marched off to find a hemp buyer. Elway himself looked pleased, and it was clear that Mama's cooking had put some meat on his bones.

"Lordy, lordy, for sure I never figured to see the two of you way out here!" Tyler blurted.

"You remember how I craved to go with you," Lucas reminded him. "Craved it so bad that as soon as we put crops in this spring—after we hadn't heard a word from you—Elway and me decided to come looking for you."

Lucas glanced admiringly first at the captain of the *Undaunted* and then at Elway. Like Rosa Lee, it was plain that he'd taken a shine to his stepfather.

"And guess what, Ty? Next year, Elway and Captain Sykes say maybe I can hire on as a cabin boy!"

"You see, Lucas didn't insist on bringing along a dog with the eyes of a born killer," Captain Sykes murmured, smiling down at Sooner. "Didn't tell me any tales about selling a load of hemp for top dollar, either. However, Mr. Snepp said it was all true, that you and your friend did indeed harvest a crop for him, and he'd paid you your share. Reckon that means I owe you an apology."

Tyler glanced at the rifle in the crook of Elway's arm. "I see you're the one that bought the Winchester off Captain Little." The sight of it pinched his heart. He'd lost it, and it was Elway himself who had to retrieve it— for twice what it was worth, if you please.

"Don't feel bad about what happened, son," Elway said gently. "I heard about it from the wharfmaster. No way could you have hung on to it, considering the pickle you were in. Our only hope, Lucas's and mine, was just to find you alive."

What funny ways the world had of turning on its axis—not in tidy ellipses the way it was supposed to, but up and down and sideways! I went off to Texas to find Papa, and Lucas and Elway came to Montana Territory to find me, Tyler mused. His chest filled up with something bigger than love. It felt as rich and timeless as the dark river that lapped against the side of the *Undaunted*. "Well, you found me," Tyler said, "and Isaac, too. So what d'you aim to do now?"

Lucas glanced up at Captain Sykes again, whose former broodiness seemed to have been replaced permanently with a fond smile. Tyler observed, however, that it was genuine fondness, not the fake kind that poor old Richard Little had bestowed on him and Isaac.

"Now that Lucas and me know you boys are safe, I reckon we'll head downriver with Cap'n Sykes when he leaves tomorrow. Our new hemp crop will need tending to, and your mama and Rosa Lee and the other boys are waiting on us," Elway said. Then Lucas laid his hand on Tyler's arm. "Why don't you come along, Ty? Isaac, too!" he cried. "It'll be the three of us again, like it used to be when we were all together back at Sweet Creek."

Tyler and Isaac exchanged glances. Without planning to, they began to laugh. So much had happened, they knew nothing would ever again be like it used to be.

"Thank you mightily for the offer, Lucas, but Isaac and me got us a pair of good horses, and we're going to head cross-country out there to California." Tyler hesitated and looked regretfully at the Winchester.

"I gave it to you once, son, and I'd be pleased to give it to you again," Elway said, as if he understood that Tyler could never ask for it. He winked. (Elway actually winked!) "When you find gold out there in California, you can pay me back."

As Elway held the rifle out to Tyler, the wharfmaster hurried up again, rattling more sheaves of paper. "Thank goodness I found you, young man," he said breathlessly. "One of the brothers from yonder at the mission just sent word that your uncle passed on shortly after your visit this morning. He was sure you'd want to know."

"Uncle?" Lucas gasped. "You mean Uncle Matt came lookin' for you, too, Ty? Did he bring Cousin Clayton with him?"

Tyler explained the lie he'd made up about being the

captain's nephew. He ended up telling Lucas, Elway, and Captain Sykes more about Richard Little than they wanted to know. When he was finished, Captain Sykes murmured, "He was the one I meant when I said some ships carried contraband. Believe me, I'd have warned you away from him if I'd suspected he'd trade off two boys to save his own worthless hide."

In the morning, before Lucas and Captain Sykes were due to head downriver, a procession including Tyler, Isaac, Lucas, Captain Sykes, and four brothers from the mission trekked up the hill on the west side of the Missouri. Sooner, whose leg still gave him fits, followed slowly behind the wood cart that carried Captain Little's canvas-wrapped body. The old man was laid to rest in a corner of the cemetery set aside for the unchurched, then the brothers covered it with dark prairie soil.

"God rest his soul," Captain Sykes murmured as a light wind moved the grass along the bluff and stirred a patch of black-eyed daisies nearby. Tyler vowed that if by chance he ever came across Mark and Paul and William, he'd tell them their father was thinking of them at the end. In far-away Brazil, Black Jack Bohannon's last thoughts had been of his family, too.

Tyler and Isaac hugged Lucas hard, knowing it would be a long while before they met again. There were handshakes with Captain Sykes and Elway, and thanks to the brothers from the mission. Lucas and the captain rode down the hill in the back of the empty wagon, while Tyler and Isaac waited on the bluff above Fort Benton to watch the *Undaunted* steam away from the levee an hour later. The wake of the ship set the *Darlin' Nell* to rocking fiercely, then she lapsed back into lonesome idleness.

Tyler mounted Mouse. Isaac climbed aboard Buddy. In the same pocket that held Papa's last letter, Many Horses's speckled stone was as warm as a beating heart. But before he could press his heels against Mouse's belly, Isaac rested his hands across the neck of his horse and announced, "First we got some bizness to take care of, Ty."

"Business?" Tyler echoed. The words sounded familiar. Yes, they were the very ones he'd used to Isaac before they divvied up Elway's money back in St. Joe.

"You sure you want me to come wit' you?" Isaac asked.

Tyler stared at him. "Why wouldn't I?"

"Because you got pretty peeved wit' me when we was livin' back there in Iron Shell's camp," Isaac reminded him. "Sometimes you was mad enough to pound ol' Isaac's head wit' a rock. You figgered your daddy was right to go off and fight agin the Union, that given a chance, black folks got mighty uppity. Tell me, ain't that the Lord's truth?"

Tyler felt his cheeks get warm. "Shoot! You been right about lots of things, Isaac, and you're right about that, too," he confessed. "The shoe was on the other foot, just like you said. But it fits a little better now—so if you can forget I was wrong, I'll try to forget Iron Shell reckoned you were the best treasure that ever came his way."

Isaac grinned. "Let's go, then," he said.

"Sooner!" Tyler called. "Oh, *Soooner!*" The red dog left his careful inspection of the fresh dark earth mounded over Captain Little's grave, and ran toward them. His limp was less noticeable once he'd worked the morning kinks out of his bones. "We're headin' west," Tyler said, "out there to where the sun goes down."

After . . .

In 1868, Chief Red Cloud signed a treaty with the whites at Fort Laramie. President Ulysses S. Grant promised the Indians that from that day forward, the Great Sioux Reservation would be "set aside for the absolute and undisturbed use and occupation of the Indians." No white person "would be permitted to pass over, settle upon, of reside in the territory."

Six years later, in 1874, General George Armstrong Custer led an expedition into the Black Hills, which was part of the Great Sioux Reservation. He confirmed the rumors about rich deposits of gold in the area. Although the Paha Sapa—the Hills That Are Black—were a spiritual sanctuary for members of the Seven Council Fires, gold miners and homesteaders ignored President Grant's promise and poured into Indian country by the thousands.

The intrusion enraged the Indians, especially chiefs such as Sitting Bull and Crazy Horse, who believed the People had been betrayed. It should have surprised no one that two years later, on a hot, windless afternoon in June 1876, General George Armstrong Custer and his Seventh Cavalry were wiped out by the Sioux near a river in southeastern Montana called the Little Bighorn. The bloody tragedy was known ever after as the Custer Massacre.

Although the Sioux had been victorious over Custer and his men, the massacre became a tragedy for them, too. By 1890, all tribes belonging to the Seven Council Fires had been pushed onto smaller reservations with names like Standing Rock, Pine Ridge, and Rosebud, to live on patches of poor land that whites didn't want for themselves.

The buffalo herds, upon which Indian life had depended, vanished. They were replaced by the white man's beef cattle. The prairie was plowed under and planted with crops such as wheat, corn, oats, flax, and barley. Soon, roads crisscrossed the plains, then railroads were built to take homesteaders' crops to market. After being bypassed by rail traffic, wild river towns like Fort Benton became sleepy little villages.

To the west, in the land the sun went down, Tyler Bohannon and Isaac Peerce discovered a different kind of gold than was buried in the Paha Sapa: the golden bounty of the new orange groves of California. What became of the girl once called Mary Burden, however, is not known. . . .